The Boy Who Could Fly

飛翔吧，男孩

原著 David A. Hill
譯者 李俊忠

About This Book

For the Student Listen to the story and do some activities on your Audio CD.
Talk about the story.

For the Teacher

Go to our Readers Resource site for information on using readers and downloadable Resource Sheets, photocopiable Worksheets, and Tapescripts. www.helblingreaders.com

For lots of great ideas on using Graded Readers consult Reading Matters, the Teacher's Guide to using Helbling Readers.

Structures

Sequencing of future tenses	Could / was able to / managed to
Present perfect plus yet, already, just	Had to / didn't have to
First conditional	Shall / could for offers
Present and past passive	May / can / could for permission Might for future possibility
How long?	Make and let
Very / really / quite	Causative have Want / ask / tell someone to do something

Structures from lower levels are also included.

Contents

Meet the Author

Hello, David. Can you tell us a little about yourself?

Yes, certainly. I was born in Walsall, UK, and after school trained[1] and worked as a teacher in England. In 1977 I left the UK, and since then I have lived in Italy, Serbia[2] and Hungary. I have also worked with students and teachers in 30 other countries around the world. These days I spend my time writing educational books, including original and adapted readers like this one, and training teachers of English. When I'm not working, I play in a blues[3] band and study the natural world and art and architecture[4]. I also read a lot and write short stories and poetry[5].

Where did you get the idea for this story?

I have always loved birds and the beauty of their flight. One of my oldest hobbies[6] is birdwatching[7], and I have always thought how wonderful it would be to be able to fly. The story began by thinking about what flying would be like for a person with wings, and then what problems someone who could fly might have.

What is the message of this story?

The message underneath[8] this story is that people must be allowed to be different, and that we should be happy that there are differences. Differences are what make the world an interesting place. It is also important that we include people who are different, and accept them and make them welcome, while respecting their individuality[9].

1 train [tren] (v.) 受訓
2 Serbia [ˋsɝbɪə] (n.) 塞爾維亞
3 blues [bluz] (n.) 爵士音樂；藍調
4 architecture [ˋɑrkə,tɛktʃɚ] (n.) 建築
5 poetry [ˋpoɪtrɪ] (n.)〔總稱〕詩
6 hobby [ˋhɑbɪ] (n.) 興趣；嗜好
7 birdwatching [ˋbɝdwɑtʃɪŋ] (n.) 賞鳥
8 underneath [,ʌndɚˋniθ] (prep.) 在表面下的……
9 individuality [,ɪndə,vɪdʒʊˋælətɪ] (n.) 個體性

Before Reading

1 There are around 9,700 different kinds of birds in the world today. They are all very different from each other in size, shape, the food they eat, the places they live, and the things they can do. Look at the pictures of these four birds. What do you know about them? How are they different from each other? Discuss with a partner.

a Emperor Penguin

b House Sparrow

c Eagle Owl

d Ostrich

2 Answer these questions:

a Which bird lives near people?
b Which bird runs very fast?
c Which bird lives in a cold climate?
d Which bird flies at night?
e Which bird eats fish?
f Which bird eats meat?
g Which bird can swim underwater?
h Which birds cannot fly?

3 Most birds can fly. In order to do this, birds have different bodies from other living creatures. They have very light bones, and very big chest muscles to move their wings up and down. They also have things which other living creatures don't have: wings and feathers. Label these two pictures.

a ____________ b ____________

4 People have always wanted to fly. What do you know about the history of human flight? Match the people (a-c) with the actions (1-3).

1 Studied flight and made drawings of different kinds of flying machines.

2 Made the first manned flight at Kittyhawk in the USA in 1903.

3 The father made wings for his son, but he flew too close to the sun, and the wax that held the feathers onto his arms melted, and the son fell into the sea.

_____ a Daedalus and Icarus
_____ b Leonardo da Vinci
_____ c Orville and Wilbur Wright

5 Which one of the three sets of people and events above did not really exist?

6 Look at this picture of the man who could fly. Write a description of him. Think about how he is different from you and describe the differences.

7 How do you think it feels to be able to fly like a bird? What would be the advantages and disadvantages? Make some notes below.

Advantages	Disadvantages
....	....
....	....
....	....
....	....

8 Discuss your ideas with a partner.

9 The main character in the story is Michael Broad – he is 'the boy who could fly'. He is the only person in the world who has wings and can fly. Read this extract from Chapter 2:

> Nobody knew where Michael came from. Sarah and George Broad, who owned a small shop, found him on the doorstep of their house one morning. He was in a basket, with a bag of new clothes and some baby food. Sarah guessed he was about nine months old. Later she found a piece of paper in the bag. The name Michael was written on it.

Where do you think Michael came from? How could he grow wings and fly? Give reasons for your answers.

10 In pairs look at these pictures from the story. Describe the setting of each one. What is happening in each picture? Choose one and write a detailed description. Try to imagine what happens next.

11 Listen to this extract from the story. Draw the route the three men took on the map.

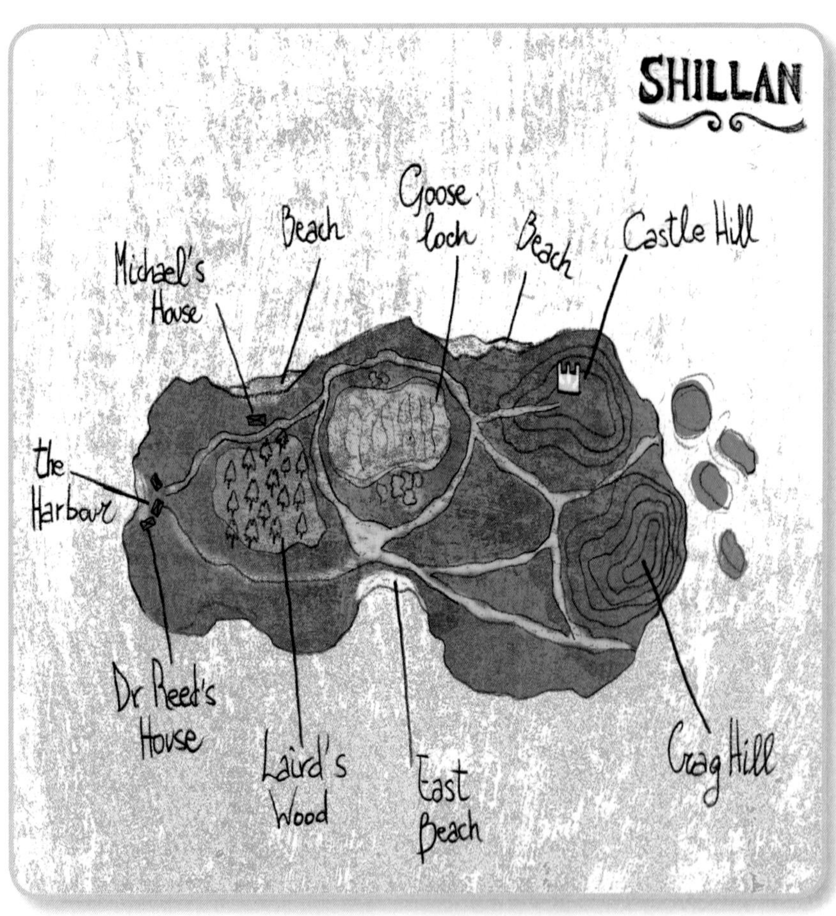

12 Now answer these questions:

- (a) Who are the three men?
- (b) Did they kill Michael?
- (c) What did they do with him?

13 Why do you think the men want to capture Michael? With a partner discuss possible reasons. Think of the following:

What ability makes Michael special?

How can the men use this ability?

Today

One hundred meters above the earth, the man who could fly moved his large white wings gently backwards and forwards[1].

It was very quiet up there, and the air was clean and fresh. When he looked down, he could see the village where he lived and the school where he taught. If he turned his head, he could see the park and, beyond that, fields[2] with cows and sheep in them.

He moved his wings a little faster and rose[3] higher. He could see even more now – those hills in the distance[4] were the Bellock Hills. And that large blue shape was Willtery Lake.

Then he began to feel a bit dizzy[5] and sick. He could fly quite easily at this height, but looking down at the ground so far below him always made him feel strange. Sometimes he was afraid of falling, but of course he never did. Birds don't fall to the ground, and he was like a bird.

He took one last look at the countryside, then he opened his wings wide, made a few slow circles[6] and gracefully[7] flew down towards[8] the park below.

He landed[9] easily on his feet. After folding[10] his wings flat[11] onto his back, he put on his special extra[12]-large jacket to cover them. Now he looked the same as everyone else. As he walked home across the grass[13], he thought about his supper.

Flying always gave him a good appetite[14].

1 backwards and forwards 來回地
2 field [fild] (n.) 田野
3 rise [raɪz] (v.) 上升
4 distance [ˋdɪstəns] (n.) 遠處
5 dizzy [ˋdɪzɪ] (a.) 頭暈的
6 circle [ˋsɝkḷ] (n.) 圓圈
7 gracefully [ˋgresfəlɪ] (adv.) 優雅地
8 towards [təˋwɔrdz] (prep.) 朝向
9 land [lænd] (v.) 降落
10 fold [fold] (v.) 交疊
11 flat [flæt] (adv.) 平直地
12 extra [ˋɛkstrə] (pref.) 超出的
13 grass [græs] (n.) 草地
14 appetite [ˋæpə͵taɪt] (n.) 食慾

How it all started

4

Nobody knew where Michael came from. Sarah and George Broad, who owned[1] a small shop, found him on the doorstep[2] of their house one morning. He was in a basket with a bag of new clothes and some baby food. Sarah guessed he was about nine months old. Later she found a piece of paper in the bag. The name *Michael* was written on it.

The Broads immediately told the police about the baby. Michael's picture and details were soon in all the papers and he was even on the national news. But nobody recognized[3] him or came to take him back, so the Broads looked after him and a year later they adopted[4] him.

Michael was happy with Sarah and George. And they were happy with him. They didn't have any children so he became the son they never had.

Michael grew up to be a nice boy. He was very popular with the customers[5] in the Broads' shop, and with his friends and teachers at his nursery school[6]. When he was old enough to understand, Sarah and George explained to him that they weren't his real parents, but he didn't mind[7].

Like all children, Michael grew taller and stronger every day. He was a normal child in every way, except for the size of his chest[8]. His chest was very large. And it grew larger and stronger as he got older. People began to notice it. The teachers began to talk about it. The Broads began to wonder[9] about it.

Adoption

- The following people all have one thing in common: they were adopted. Do you know why they are famous? Discuss with a partner.

Aristotle	*Edgar Allan Poe*
Charles Dickens	*John Lennon*
Crazy Horse	*Nelson Mandela*

- See if you can discover the names of other famous adopted people or adoptive parents.

1 own [on] (v.) 擁有
2 doorstep [ˋdor,stɛp] (n.) 門階
3 recognize [ˋrɛkəg,naɪz] (v.) 認出
4 adopt [əˋdɑpt] (v.) 收養
5 customer [ˋkʌstəmɚ] (n.) 顧客
6 nursery school 托兒所；育幼院
7 mind [maɪnd] (v.) 介意
8 chest [tʃɛst] (n.) 胸膛
9 wonder [ˋwʌndɚ] (v.) 想知道

Going to school

5 Michael's life changed when he started primary school[1]. He started feeling pains[2] in his back, near his shoulders. Sometimes he couldn't sleep at night because of them. The family doctor examined[3] him but he found nothing unusual.

When Michael started his second year at school the pains got much worse, so Sarah took him to see a specialist[4] at the hospital. The specialist examined him and ordered[5] x-rays[6]. From the x-rays he could clearly see that some extra[7] bones were growing out of Michael's shoulders. These bones were pushing against his skin and causing[8] the pains. The doctor told Sarah to bring him back the following[9] day, but it was too late.

That night Sarah and George were woken up by shouts from Michael's bedroom. They quickly ran to him and were shocked by what they saw. A large bone was growing out of each of his shoulders!

George called an ambulance, and an hour later Michael was back in the hospital. They x-rayed him again and several specialists examined him. George and Sarah stayed there all night and were able to see him from time to time[10]. Between visits, the specialists asked them a lot of questions about Michael. At seven o'clock in the morning a nurse told them to go home.

'What about Michael?' asked George.

'He has to stay here,' the nurse replied.

1 primary school 小學
2 pain [pen] (n.) 痛；痛苦
3 examine [ɪg`zæmɪn] (v.) 檢查；診察
4 specialist [`spɛʃəlɪst] (n.) 專科醫生
5 order [`ɔrdɚ] (v.) 醫囑
6 x-ray [`ɛks`re] (n.) X 光
7 extra [`ɛkstrə] (a.) 額外的
8 cause [kɔz] (v.) 引起；導致
9 following [`fɑləwɪŋ] (a.) 接下來的
10 from time to time 三不五時地

Michael alone

6 Later that same morning he was put into an ambulance and taken to another hospital a long way away.

That day he cried because of the pains in his shoulders. He cried because he didn't know where he was. He cried because he wanted Sarah and George.

Everyone in the hospital was very nice to him. They gave him his favorite food, read him stories and let him watch television. But he was still very sad. In the evening he talked to Sarah on the phone.

'Don't worry, Michael,' she said. 'We'll come and see you tomorrow.'

Michael stayed in this special hospital for a year. The bones in his shoulders grew bigger, and new muscles[1] developed[2] around them. After the first six months white feathers[3] started to grow on the bones, and it was clear to everyone, including Michael, that they were wings. Slowly he found he could move the new bones by using the muscles in his chest.

Every morning a team of doctors examined him. Then in the afternoons other doctors tried to help him to remember his past, before Sarah found him. But he couldn't remember anything. Michael didn't like staying at the hospital. The only things he liked were the lessons he had with his teacher, Mr. Smith, and the visits from George and Sarah on Sundays.

1 muscle [ˋmʌsl̩] (n.) 肌肉
2 develop [dɪˋvɛləp] (v.) 發展
3 feather [ˋfɛðɚ] (n.) 羽毛
4 suit [sut] (n.)（一套）衣服
5 expert [ˋɛkspɚt] (n.) 專家
6 flight [flaɪt] (n.) 飛行

Mr Smith was a small dark man in a grey suit[4]. He didn't teach much Maths or English. Most of the lessons were about flying because Mr Smith was really an expert[5] on flight[6].

He explained the history of flight to Michael, from Leonardo Da Vinci's experiments with flying machines[7] to modern jet[8] engines[9]. Michael learnt about birds, bats, insects and flying animals. He learnt about how the air moves, and what winds are. He drew[10] models[11] and diagrams[12]. He watched films[13] and did experiments. Soon Michael became an expert, too.

He also had to do exercises in the gym[14] every afternoon. A big man called Pete showed him what to do, but Mr Smith and one of the doctors always watched and took notes[15]. The exercises he did were to make his chest and new wing muscles stronger. At first they were very difficult to do, but gradually[16] they became easier.

Away from home

- Have you ever been away from home without your family? When was it? How did you feel? Share with a friend.
- How do you think Michael feels?

7 machine [məˋʃin] (n.) 機器
8 jet [dʒɛt] (n.) 噴射機
9 engine [ˋɛndʒən] (n.) 引擎
10 draw [drɔ] (v.) 畫；繪製
11 model [ˋmɑdḷ] (n.) 模型
12 diagram [ˋdaɪə͵græm] (n.) 圖表；圖解
13 film [fɪlm] (n.) 影片
14 gym [dʒɪm] (n.) 健身房
15 take notes 記筆記
16 gradually [ˋgrædʒʊəlɪ] (adv.) 漸漸地

1 suddenly [ˋsʌdn̩lɪ] (adv.) 突然地
2 meter [ˋmitɚ] (n.) 公尺
3 amazing [əˋmezɪŋ] (a.) 令人吃驚的
4 properly [ˋprɑpɚlɪ] (adv.) 正確地
5 realize [ˋrɪə͵laɪz] (v.) 了解到
6 bench [bɛntʃ] (n.) 長椅

Michael flies

And then one day, nine months after Michael arrived at the special hospital, he flew for the first time. His wings were now covered with beautiful, long, white feathers. He was in the gym doing his exercises, when suddenly[1] he rose into the air. Michael was so surprised that he stopped moving his wings and he fell to the ground.

'Try again,' Pete said. So he tried again and . . . YES . . . he could fly!!

At first, he could only lift himself a meter[2] or two off the ground and stay there for about a minute. Then he had to rest. But his muscles got stronger, and, after a month, he could stay in the air for several minutes. It was an amazing[3] feeling!

After that, Pete started taking Michael outside for his lessons and soon Michael learnt how to fly properly[4]. He felt sorry for Mr Smith. His teacher knew so much about flying but couldn't actually do it himself, and he, a seven-year-old boy, could! Michael suddenly realized[5] that he was different and special. He was the boy who could fly. Perhaps the *only* boy in the world who could fly.

The following Sunday Michael asked the nurses to take George and Sarah to a quiet little garden next to the hospital building. They were sitting on a bench[6] waiting for him when, suddenly, he ran into the middle of the grass.

'Hi, Sarah! Hi, George!' he shouted. 'Watch me!'

He moved his big, white-feathered wings and slowly rose up in the air. Sarah and George couldn't believe their eyes! They were laughing and crying at the same time.

Escape from the hospital

9 Michael was tired of[1] being in the hospital. He wanted to go home, and Sarah and George wanted him back.

'Why?' he shouted. 'Why do I have to be here? I'm sick of[2] living in a hospital. I can fly. So what?[3] Let me go home!'

But every day the doctors found another reason for him to stay there.

'They'll never let me go home,' he thought. 'I'll become like a rare[4] animal in a zoo. I'll be "the flying boy".' And he felt very unhappy. The Broads were unhappy too. They didn't want Michael to stay in the hospital for the rest of his life. They wanted him to be like other boys of his age. So the next time that Sarah and George went to see Michael, the three of them made a plan.

The plan

- What is Michael, George and Sarah's plan? Make groups of 3. Each person is one of the characters. Together discuss ways to get Michael out of the hospital.
- Find the pros and cons of each idea. Try and find an idea that will work.

1 be tired of 厭倦了……
2 be sick of 厭倦了……
3 So what? 那又不是什麼問題！
4 rare [rɛr] (a.) 稀有的
5 porter [`portɚ] (n.) 門房
6 land [lænd] (v.) 降落
7 press [prɛs] (v.) 壓
8 accelerator [ək`sɛlə,retɚ] (n.) 油門
9 race [res] (v.) 全速行進

10 The following Sunday morning, George and Sarah drove to the hospital to visit Michael as usual. Sarah got out of the car and went inside, but George didn't. He stayed in the car park. Sarah went into the garden where Michael joined her. After a few minutes she went back inside. 'I forgot my glasses,' she said to the porter[5]. 'They're in the car.'

The porter unlocked the door and let her out. Sarah walked to the car park and got into the car. A moment later, Michael flew over the high hospital wall, landed[6] in the car park, folded his wings, and got into the car too. George pressed[7] his foot on the accelerator[8] and they raced[9] down the road away from the hospital.

Problems at home

11 The porter at the hospital rang[1] the police. And someone at the police station rang the newspapers. When George arrived home, the car was immediately surrounded[2] by photographers[3] and reporters[4] from every newspaper and television and radio station in the country. It was impossible for the three of them to get out of the car without being attacked[5] by the journalists[6] and paparazzi[7]. They were shouting:

'Can you give us some idea of the boy's mental[8] state, Mrs Broad ?'

'Mr Broad, who do you think the boy's real mother is?'

'Hey, Michael! What's flying like?'

'Michael, what are you hoping to do now?'

Michael, Sarah and George had to fight their way through the crowd[9] into their house. They were very frightened. The telephone kept ringing, people kept knocking on the front door and some cameramen[10] even went into the back garden and started taking photographs of the house. Sarah closed the curtains. They stood and looked at each other. It was not a happy homecoming[11] for Michael.

'What shall we do, George?' Sarah asked her husband.

'I don't know,' he answered.

Suddenly there was a very loud knock at the front door and a voice shouted:

'Open the door, please, Mr Broad. Police!'

1 ring [rɪŋ] (v.)〔英〕打電話
2 surround [səˋraʊnd] (v.) 圍繞
3 photographer [fəˋtɑgrəfɚ] (n.) 攝影師
4 reporter [rɪˋportɚ] (n.) 記者
5 attack [əˋtæk] (v.) 襲擊
6 journalist [ˋdʒɝnəlɪst] (n.) 新聞記者
7 paparazzi [ˏpɑpəˋrɑtsɪ] (n.)〔複〕狗仔隊（其單數為 paparazzo [ˏpɑpəˋrɑtso]）
8 mental [ˋmɛntl̩] (a.) 精神的；心理的
9 crowd [kraʊd] (n.) 人群
10 cameraman [ˋkæmərəˏmæn] (n.) 攝影記者
11 homecoming [ˋhomˏkʌmɪŋ] (n.) 返家

12 When George opened it, he saw two tall policemen, a plain clothes[1] inspector[2] and one of the doctors from the hospital. Other policemen were pushing all the media[3] people back into the street.

George let the inspector and the doctor into the house but the two uniformed policemen stayed outside.

'What you did was very wrong,' the doctor said. 'We told you Michael couldn't go home.'

'But he was tired of being in the hospital,' said Sarah. 'He needs to be at home with us, living a normal life – going to school, playing with his friends . . .'

'I know, Mrs Broad,' answered the doctor. 'But Michael isn't a normal child. You saw what happened outside. He needs to be protected[4] from the world.'

'But I don't want to live in a hospital for the rest of my life,' shouted Michael. 'I'm not ill. I want to live like other children.'

Michael's future

- What do you think Michael's parents, the doctor and the police inspector decide?
- Imagine you are each of the following people. What do you think is the best for Michael?

Sarah Broad	*George Broad*
Michael's doctor	*The policeman*

Yes, I know, Michael,' said the doctor. 'But we need to protect you from people like those reporters, and anyone else who might want to use you and hurt you.'

'Hurt him?' asked George. 'But he's just a little boy.'

'Yes, he is,' answered the doctor. 'The only little boy in the world with a pair of wings! We want to make sure that nothing bad happens to him.'

'You just want to keep him in that hospital so that you can study him!' said Sarah. 'You aren't interested in him as a person.'

'In one way you are right, Mrs Broad,' said the doctor. 'Michael is very unusual and scientists[5] from all over the world are interested in his development[6]. But I can assure you that we *are* concerned[7] about him as a person.'

The Broads talked to the doctor and the police inspector all evening. Michael went to his bedroom and tried to sleep while plans for his future[8] were made downstairs.

1 plain clothes 便衣
2 inspector [ɪn`spɛktɚ] (n.) 檢查員；視察員
3 media [`midɪə] (n.)〔複〕媒體（單數為 medium）
4 protect [prə`tɛkt] (v.) 保護
5 scientist [`saɪəntɪst] (n.) 科學家
6 development [dɪ`vɛləpmənt] (n.) 發展；生長
7 concerned [kən`sɝnd] (a.) 關心的
8 future [`fjutʃɚ] (n.) 未來

A change

14 Early the next morning, Mr Broad walked round to the local[1] newsagent's[2] to buy his morning paper[3].

'Good morning, John,' he said to the newsagent.

'Morning, George,' the man replied, smiling. 'How does it feel to be famous?'

'What do you mean?' asked George, very surprised.

'Well, look at the front pages of all the papers!' answered the newsagent. 'And I saw you on the TV last night.'

George looked at the national[4] papers on the shelves[5] and saw pictures of himself, his wife and Michael everywhere, and big headlines[6] that said: MICHAEL FLIES HOME and SUPERBOY HOME AT LAST!

'Michael's a famous star now,' said the newsagent. 'You'll soon be a very rich man, George.'

'Oh, shut up, John!' replied George angrily. 'And give me one copy of[7] all today's papers, please.'

When George got home, the first reporters were already outside the house. They fired[8] question after question at him:

'What plans have you got for Michael today, Mr Broad?'

'When can we see Michael fly?'

'How does it feel to have such an unusual son?'

George ignored[9] them.

1 local [ˋlokḷ] (a.) 當地的
2 newsagent [ˋnjuz͵edʒənt] (n.) 〔英〕報紙的經銷商
3 paper [ˋpepɚ] (n.) 報紙
4 national [ˋnæʃənḷ] (a.) 全國性的
5 shelf [ʃɛlf] (n.) 架子
6 headline [ˋhɛd͵laɪn] (n.) 頭條新聞
7 a copy of 一份……
8 fire [faɪr] (v.) 連珠炮地發問
9 ignore [ɪgˋnor] (v.) 忽視；不理會

15 'Look at this!' he said to Sarah, and put the papers on the kitchen table. 'There are pictures and stories about us everywhere.'

'Oh, no!' she said unhappily.

During breakfast they talked to Michael about the plans for his future.

Later in the morning, two doctors arrived. They took Michael through the crowd of reporters, who were still shouting questions and taking photos, to an ambulance and he was driven back to the hospital.

Michael stayed there for a month. And then, one Monday morning, the police car that Michael was expecting[1] came to collect[2] him. A policeman put his luggage[3] in the boot[4] and then got in the back seat with him. They drove all day, stopping only once for something to eat. At about five o'clock, Michael saw a sign that said 'Scotland[5]', then, an hour or two later, he saw the sea. The car stopped in a lonely place on the coast[6] where a boat was waiting for them. He and the policeman got on it. It was his first time on a boat and he felt quite excited.

Michael was on his way to an island which was an hour's boat-ride from the coast. The name of the island was Shillan. George and Sarah were waiting for him there. They were all very happy as they walked towards the house that was their new home. Inside, the Broads showed Michael around. His bedroom was very big with lovely views of the sea. All his toys and books were already there.

For the first time in many months, he felt really happy.

1 expect [ɪk`spɛkt] (v.) 期待
2 collect [kə`lɛkt] (v.) 接走
3 luggage [`lʌgɪdʒ] (n.) 行李（不可數）
4 boot [but] (n.)〔英〕行李箱
5 Scotland [`skɑtlənd] (n.) 蘇格蘭
6 coast [kost] (n.) 海岸

Life on Shillan

16 The next morning at 7.30, Michael's new life began. He got up and had his breakfast in the big warm kitchen with George and Sarah. At 9 o'clock, a doctor called Richard Reed came to the house and took him to a laboratory[7] that was full of special equipment[8]. Dr Reed photographed, weighed[9] and measured[10] Michael and recorded everything on a computer.

At 9.30, Michael was taken to a room where there were books, paper, paints, tools, science equipment, a computer, a TV and DVD player, and a nice big desk.

'This is your classroom,' the doctor said.

Michael sat at the desk and Dr Reed showed him how to switch[11] on the computer.

'Now put on[12] the headset[13] and go to Channel 10,' said the doctor.

Michael clicked[14] on the Channel 10 icon. Two people sitting at a desk appeared[15] on the screen.

'Good morning, Michael,' they both said.

7 laboratory [ˋlæbrə,torɪ] (n.) 實驗室
8 equipment [ɪˋkwɪpmənt] (n.) 設備
9 weigh [we] (v.) 稱重量
10 measure [ˋmɛʒɚ] (v.) 測量
11 switch [swɪtʃ] (v.) 開或關
12 put on 戴上
13 headset [ˋhɛd,sɛt] (n.) 戴在頭上的耳機
14 click [klɪk] (v.) 點擊
15 appear [əˋpɪr] (v.) 出現

17 'My name's Sally Roberts,' said the lady, smiling. 'And this is Paul Brown. We're your teachers. You can use the microphone[1] on your headset to talk to us.'

Every day one or both teachers told him what to do. He did Maths, English, History, and all the other school subjects[2]. He emailed his work to Sally or Paul and they talked about it and helped him if he had problems.

School

- What do you study at school?
- Are all your subjects compulsory[3] or can you choose some of them?
- Would you like to study like Michael?

At 11.15 he had a drink and some biscuits in the kitchen with Sarah and George. Then he did some more lessons until one o'clock. After lunch, if the weather was good, he went out for a walk.

Michael usually liked going for walks on his own, but sometimes Sarah and George went with him. Twice a week he had to do a Biology[4] project about the island and send a report[5] to his teachers the following morning.

1 microphone [ˋmaɪkrəˏfon] (n.) 麥克風
2 subject [ˋsʌbdʒɪkt] (n.) 學科
3 compulsory [kəmˋpʌlsərɪ] (a.) 必修的
4 biology [baɪˋɑlədʒɪ] (n.) 生物學
5 report [rɪˋport] (n.) 報告
6 do exercises 做運動

Later in the afternoon, Dr Reed returned to the Broads' house and they went to a room where there was a small gym. From four to four thirty every day Michael had to do exercises[6], which Dr Reed filmed[7]. Sometimes they were exercises like all children do at school, but other times the doctor made him do special exercises to make his wings and chest muscles strong.

In the evenings he played computer games, watched TV, played cards or other games with Sarah and George, or read books from the library in the classroom.

Shillan was a small island. At the southern end there was a little harbor[8] where boats arrived. The cottage[9] where Dr Reed lived was there, too. Michael's house was in the east of the island. Behind the house there was a wood of pine trees[10] called Laird's Wood and a lake called Goose[11] Loch. In winter many ducks and geese came to swim and feed[12] on the lake. The southern part of Shillan was quite flat[13] and covered with grass, but the north was hilly. In the northwest there were two hills: Castle Hill, which got its name from a ruined[14] castle that stood on the top it, and Crag Hill, which was very rocky. Lots of wild flowers grew on the island – some of them were quite rare.

7 film [fɪlm] (v.) 拍影片
8 harbor [ˋharbɚ] (n.) 港口
9 cottage [ˋkatɪdʒ] (n.) 小屋
10 pine tree 松樹

11 goose [gus] (n.) 鵝（複數為 geese [gis]）
12 feed [fid] (v.) 餵養；吃
13 flat [flæt] (a.) 平坦的
14 ruined [ˋruɪnd] (a.) 毀壞的

19 Soon Michael knew every centimeter[1] of the island and he could recognize most of the flowers, birds and animals that lived there. At first he missed the company of other children, but as time passed he got used to playing by himself.

Sarah and George loved their new life. They no longer had to work in the shop and had time for their hobbies. George grew[2] vegetables in the garden and Sarah painted pictures of wild flowers. When she wasn't painting or doing housework, she made clothes for Michael. Sarah designed[3] an extra-large jacket for him, which was easy to put on and which covered his wings.

1 centimeter [ˋsɛntə͵mitɚ] (n.) 公分
2 grow [gro] (v.) 種植
3 design [dɪˋzaɪn] (v.) 設計

And sometimes Michael flew. He could fly from his house to the north end of the island in fifteen minutes. As he got better at it, he flew higher and for a longer time. One Saturday when he was eight years old he came home at lunchtime and said, 'Guess what, George! I flew all round the coast of the island this morning! I had to stop four times, but not for very long.'

George and Sarah were surprised, but then they realized that Michael's flight was only like a long bicycle ride or a game of football for other children.

20

And so the days passed happily for the Broads and Michael. Once a month a boat came and brought them food and any other supplies[1] they needed. Otherwise they saw nobody else. They watched the seasons come and go. In winter the sea was very rough[2] and sometimes frightening[3], and it usually snowed several times. In summer the weather was often very beautiful and the days were long – it was light enough to see until ten o'clock at night.

Michael grew stronger and taller. He worked hard at his lessons and became a very clever boy. George and Sarah were pleased with their decision to move to Shillan because Michael was able to grow up out of the public eye[4].

Your home

- Where do you live? Tick (✓).
  - ☐ In a big city ☐ In a small town or village
  - ☐ In a town ☐ In the country
- With a partner discuss the advantages and disadvantages of where you live.

1 supplies [sə`plaɪz] (n.)〔複〕生活用品
2 rough [rʌf] (a.) 狂暴的
3 frightening [`fraɪtṇɪŋ] (a.) 使人驚嚇的
4 out of the public eye 避開人們的眼光

A plan

21 One evening, when Michael was twelve years old, Dr Reed came to see them. He wanted to talk about something.

'I got a phone call from my boss in London,' he said. 'The BBC have asked if they can make a film about Michael.'

Sarah looked worried. She still had bad memories of reporters, photographers and television crews[1].

'I'm not sure it's a very good idea,' she said.

'Wait a minute, Sarah,' said George. 'Let's listen to what the doctor says. Go on, Richard.'

'The producer[2] of *Strange But True* wants to include a 45-minute documentary[3] about Michael in his new series[4],' Dr Reed explained. 'My boss thinks that it might be a good idea. Michael's growing up. We can't keep him on this island forever. We need to introduce the people of Britain to him so that one day he can live a normal life somewhere – go to university, get a job and so on.'

'Well, I agree with that,' said George. 'But isn't it dangerous for him now? He's still young, after all.'

'I'd like to do it,' said Michael. 'We've seen every episode[5] of *Strange But True* on TV. It's a great program[6].'

Television

- Do you like watching television?
- What are your favorite television programs?
- Do you want to be on television?
- Do you think Michael is making the correct decision?

'Yes, it is,' agreed the doctor. 'The producers of the program are very serious people. Naturally, we'll see the film before it goes on television to make sure it's alright.'

'They can't make the film here, though. It's too dangerous,' said Sarah. 'Someone might recognize the place, and then all those newspaper reporters will come here.'

'Yes, obviously[7] they must make it somewhere else,' said Dr Reed.

'Well, I'm still not sure it's a good idea,' said Sarah, looking at George.

'Do you think it's too risky[8] for Michael, Richard?' asked George.

'No, I don't,' said Dr Reed. 'And there's another point. Quite an important one. The BBC will give Michael £10,000 if we let them make the film.'

'Wow!' said Michael. 'That means I could buy . . . I could buy . . .anything!'

'Well, actually,' said the doctor laughing. 'It isn't a bad idea for Michael to have some money in the bank for the future.'

'Yes, you're right,' said Sarah.

'So, shall I tell my boss to go ahead[9] and make the arrangements[10]?' asked Dr Reed.

The Broads looked at Michael, and then at each other. They all nodded[11] their heads.

'Right! I'll talk to him tomorrow,' said the doctor. 'And now, what about a game of cards?'

1 crew [kru] (n.) 一組工作人員
2 producer [prə`djusɚ] (n.) 製片人
3 documentary [ˏdɑkjə`mɛntərɪ] (n.) 紀錄片
4 series [`siriz] (n.) 系列節目
5 episode [`ɛpəˏsod] (n.) 連續劇的一集
6 program [`progræm] (n.) 節目
7 obviously [`ɑbvɪəslɪ] (adv.) 顯然地
8 risky [`rɪskɪ] (a.) 冒險的
9 go ahead 開始著手
10 arrangements [ə`rendʒmənts] (n.)〔複〕安排
11 nod [nɑd] (v.) 點頭

The film

23

A police helicopter[1] flew in to pick them up one morning in May. Sarah, George, Michael and Dr Reed were waiting for it in the field. They all climbed inside and it took off[2]. It was a beautiful day and the views of the mountains, lakes and river valleys were wonderful. At midday the helicopter landed at a deserted[3] airport[4].

'This was an important military[5] center, but it's not used now,' explained Dr. Reed as they walked over to some buildings. 'My boss chose it because it's a long way from Shillan and there are no people around. Also, they can film Michael flying inside the big hangars[6] where they kept the planes[7] years ago.'

The people from the BBC were already there. Dr Reed introduced everyone and then the producer of *Strange But True*, Paul Salter, invited them to have some lunch together.

'We want to film some interviews[8] with you all,' said Paul. 'There are only four of us here – Mary, who will interview you, Steve, our cameraman, Jeff, the sound and lighting[9] technician[10], and myself. We want everyone to be as relaxed as possible, so we'll do all the interviews here in this room. Later on we'll move into a hangar to film Michael flying.'

1 helicopter [ˋhɛlɪˏkɑptɚ] (n.) 直升機
2 take off 起飛
3 deserted [dɪˋzɝtɪd] (a.) 廢棄的
4 airport [ˋɛrˏport] (n.) 機場
5 military [ˋmɪləˏtɛrɪ] (a.) 軍事的
6 hangar [ˋhæŋɚ] (n.) 飛機棚
7 plane [plen] (n.)〔口〕飛機
8 interview [ˋɪntɚˏvju] (n.) 訪問
9 lighting [ˋlaɪtɪŋ] (n.)〔總稱〕舞臺燈光
10 technician [tɛkˋnɪʃən] (n.) 技師

After lunch the BBC people set up[1] their equipment. Just before they went to do the first interviews, Dr Reed turned to George, Sarah and Michael. 'Remember! Do *not* mention Shillan! Don't even say we live on an island, or that we live in Scotland. We don't want the BBC people to know where we live. OK?'

George, Sarah and Michael nodded.

During the next two days the four of them were interviewed alone, in pairs and as a group. Then, at lunchtime on the third day, Paul Salter called them all together.

'Thank you all very much,' he said. 'We've got some great interviews on film now so you can all take this afternoon off[2]. Tomorrow morning we'll go to the hangar to get some pictures of Michael in the air.'

The interview

- With a partner think of questions to ask Michael. Share them with the class and choose the best five.
- Then with your partner take turns being Michael and the interviewer and answer all of the questions.
- Act out the interviews in class.

1 set up 著手準備
2 take the afternoon off 下午休工
3 footstep [ˋfʊt͵stɛp] (n.) 腳步聲
4 warplane [ˋwɔr͵plen] (n.) 軍機
5 look forward to 期盼（後接名詞或動名詞）
6 puzzled [ˋpʌzḷd] (a.) 困惑的
7 suppose [səˋpoz] (v.) 猜想
8 expression [ɪkˋsprɛʃən] (n.) 表情

That afternoon, when the Broads were having a rest and Dr Reed was talking to Paul Salter, Michael went out for a walk. He walked over to have a closer look at the helicopter when he heard footsteps[3] behind him. It was Jeff.

'Hey, Mickey!' he said. 'What are you doing?'

'Just having a look at this helicopter,' answered Michael coldly. He didn't like being called Mickey.

'Have you seen the old planes?' Jeff was trying to be friendly.

'What planes?'

'There are some old warplanes[4] here,' Jeff said. 'Would you like to see them?'

'Yes, OK,' said Michael. 'Where are they?'

'In Number 2 hangar,' replied Jeff. 'Did you enjoy doing the interviews, Mickey?'

'Well,' said Michael. 'It was alright at first, but then it got a bit boring.'

'I expect you're looking forward to[5] tomorrow,' said the technician.

'Why?' asked Michael, puzzled[6].

'Well, you're flying tomorrow, aren't you? It's really amazing.'

'Well, I suppose[7] it is,' said Michael. 'For other people.'

'What do the kids at your school say?' asked Jeff, looking at Michael with a strange expression[8] on his face.

26 'They don't say anything,' answered Michael.

'Why's that?'

'Well, there isn't a school on Shill . . .,' Michael stopped himself before he said all of the name.

'Shill? Where's that?' asked Jeff. 'I've never heard of anywhere called Shill.'

'Er – it's – er – it's . . .,' said Michael, going very red in the face.

'Um – I have to get back now, Jeff. It's getting late.'

And he turned round and ran off leaving the technician looking at him. 'On Shill,' he said to himself. 'Hmm . . . on Shill . . .'

The filming of Michael flying in the hangar went very well. They finished in time for lunch, and at seven o'clock that evening the Broads, Michael and Dr Reed were back on the island of Shillan.

Jeff's friends

27

The phone rang in Slim Wilson's study. He switched off[1] the TV and went to answer it.

'Slim?'

'Yes?'

'It's Jeff. Jeff Hunter.'

'Hello Jeff. Any news?'

'Yes, I think I've found something out. Can I come round?'

'OK. Come at 7.30. Peters will be here.'

Jeff rang the doorbell and Wilson let him in. Peters, a large, bald-headed[2] man, was sitting on the sofa.

'Well?' asked Wilson.

'The boy is amazing, Slim,' Jeff said. 'He's exactly what we need for the job. One minute he's standing on the ground, then he moves those wings of his, and up he goes! It's incredible[3]!'

'Did you find out where he lives?' asked Peters.

'Well, it wasn't easy,' Jeff replied. 'They were extremely[4] careful. But I talked to the boy alone one day. He started to say a name, then stopped.'

'What did he say?' asked Wilson.

'He said "There isn't a school on Shill".'

'Where's Shill?' asked Wilson.

'I don't know. I asked him, but he didn't tell me,' said Jeff. 'When I got home, I looked at a map but I couldn't find it.'

1 switch off 關掉
2 bald-headed [ˋbɔldˋhɛdɪd] (a.) 禿頭的
3 incredible [ɪnˋkrɛdəbḷ] (a.) 難以置信的
4 extremely [ɪkˋstrimlɪ] (adv.) 極度的

28 Wilson went over to his bookcase and took out a big atlas[1] with detailed[2] maps of Britain[3] in it. He looked in the index[4].

'There's nowhere called Shill in Britain,' he said. 'Perhaps they live in another country.'

'Maybe, but I think it was just the first part of a longer name,' said Jeff.

Wilson looked at the index again. 'Shilbottle, Shildon, Shillan, three Shillfords, Shillingstone . . .,' he read. 'There are lots of places beginning with Shill.'

'Well, let's see where they are on the maps,' said Jeff. 'It can't be a town or a city. It must be somewhere small.'

The three men checked all the places on the maps and discussed those that seemed possible.

'Shillmoor is in the hills in the north of England,' said Jeff. 'It must be very small because it isn't on my map at home.'

'Yes, it's just two or three houses. Look.' said Peters, pointing to the map.

'And Shiltenish seems even smaller,' said Jeff. 'It's in Scotland, miles from anywhere. And then there's Shillan – an island near the west coast of Scotland.'

'What do you think, Slim?' said Peters.

'Tell me what the boy said again, Jeff,' said Wilson.

'He said, "There isn't a school on Shill . . .",' Jeff answered.

The place

- How does Wilson know that Michael is on Shillan?
- What clue does Jeff give him that tells him?

'Well, there's the answer!' said Wilson, smiling.

Jeff and Peters looked puzzled.

'What do you mean?' asked Peters.

'The boy said, 'There isn't a school *on* Shill . . .',' Wilson explained. '*On* Shill . . . Not *in* Shill. You only say *on* when you're talking about a hill or an island. Shillmoor is a village on a hill, not a hill itself. Shiltenish is on an island, not an island itself. Shillan is the name of an island. 'There's no school on *Shillan*.' That's what Michael *didn't* say!'

The other two men looked at Wilson.

'Congratulations, Sherlock Holmes!' said Peters, and they all laughed.

On an island

- Michael lives on an island. Complete the following sentences with the correct prepositions.

  a Diana wants to live ____________ London.
  b My house is ____________ the corner of the road.
  c He is waiting ____________ the bus stop.
  d My mum is ____________ home.
  e York is ____________ the north of England.
  f We are going ____________ holidays next week.
  g Their new house is ____________ the center.
  h We had a picnic ____________ that mountain.

1 atlas [ˋætləs] (n.) 地圖集
2 detailed [ˋdiˋteld] (a.) 詳細的
3 Britain [ˋbrɪtən] (n.) 英國
4 index [ˋɪndɛks] (n.) 索引

Visitors on Shillan

30

After the filming trip[1], life on Shillan returned to normal. A few weeks later a copy of the documentary arrived from the BBC. The doctor and the Broads sat down to watch it that same evening. They found it very strange to see themselves on film.

'Well done, everybody!' said Dr Reed. 'We managed to[2] do all the interviews without saying where we lived. I'll talk to my boss tomorrow and tell him we're happy for the BBC to show the film on television.'

That night three men landed on Shillan's East Beach in a small rubber[3] dinghy[4]. They hid it behind some rocks and covered it with pieces of wood that they found on the beach[5].

1 trip [trɪp] (n.) 旅行
2 manage to 設法
3 rubber [ˋrʌbɚ] (n.) 橡膠
4 dinghy [ˋdɪŋgɪ] (n.) 小艇
5 beach [bitʃ] (n.) 海灘

31 They looked at their map with a torch[1].

'Right,' said Wilson. 'We need to go north.'

Jeff Hunter looked at his compass[2]. 'This way,' he said.

They walked along the path until they came to Crag Hill, then they went west to Castle Hill.

'OK,' said Wilson. 'This is the place!'

They walked silently[3] up the side of the hill. It was just starting to get light when they got to the ruined castle on the top.

'This is a very good place,' said Peters, looking over the wall. 'We'll be able to see everything from here.'

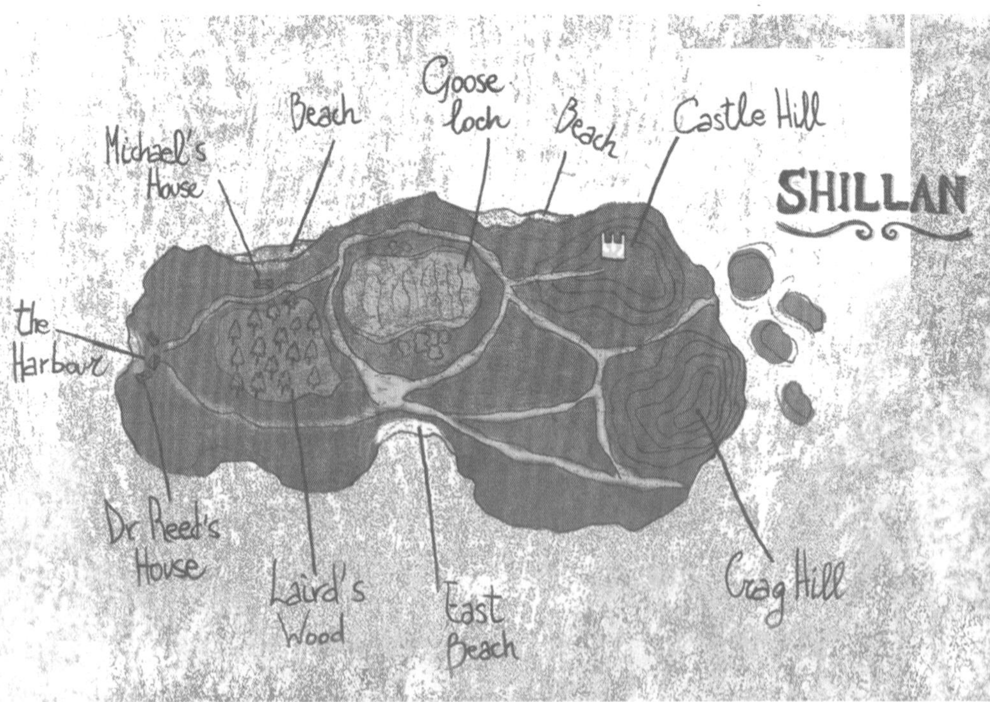

The three men

- Think. Who are the three men?
- What are they going to do? Share your ideas with a partner.

After his morning lessons Michael went down into the kitchen for lunch. Sarah was taking a fish pie out of the oven.

'Dr Reed caught the fish yesterday,' she said. 'Go and call George, please!'

After lunch, Michael got up and gave Sarah a big hug[4]. 'That was delicious!' he said. 'My compliments[5] to the chef[6]!'

Sarah laughed.

'I'm off to do my Biology homework now. See you later. Bye!' And he picked up his rucksack[7] and went out into the warm sunshine.

He took the path[8] to Goose Loch. He was doing a project on the plants that were growing in the wet grass around the lake. There were some rare species[9], and he was making a map of where they grew.

'There he is!' said Jeff to Wilson.

1 torch [tɔrtʃ] (n.) 火把
2 compass [ˋkʌmpəs] (n.) 羅盤；指南針
3 silently [ˋsaɪləntlɪ] (adv.) 寂靜地
4 hug [hʌg] (n.) 擁抱
5 compliment [ˋkɑmpləmənt] (n.) 恭維
6 chef [ʃɛf] (n.) 主廚；廚師
7 rucksack [ˋrʌk͵sæk] (n.) 帆布背包
8 path [pæθ] (n.) 小徑
9 species [ˋspiʃiz] (n.) 種類；品種

'He's walking along the path, next to the lake. Look!'

Wilson took the binoculars[1] and looked through them. He watched Michael walk to the northern end of Goose Loch.

'He's stopped,' Wilson said. 'He's taking out a book and he's writing something.'

'What do you think he's doing?' asked Peters.

'I don't know,' answered Wilson. 'I think he's making notes about something he's seen in the grass.'

They watched for a bit longer. Michael continued to write.

Suddenly Jeff said, 'OK! Are you ready?'

'Yes,' said Wilson. 'Peters, have you got the gun?'

'Yes. Here it is!' answered Peters.

'OK. Pick up your stuff[2] and let's go!'

The three men crept[3] quietly down the side of Castle Hill and across the grass towards Michael. When they were about 200 meters away from him, they stopped and lay down on the ground on their stomachs[4]. Peters got his gun ready. They waited.

1 binoculars [bɪˋnɑkjələz] (n.)〔複〕雙筒望遠鏡
2 stuff [stʌf] (n.) 物品；東西
3 creep [krip] (v.) 躡手躡足地走
4 stomach [ˋstʌmək] (n.) 胃；腹部

34

After a while, Michael put his book in his rucksack and stood up. Peters aimed[1] and fired[2]. Michael shouted with pain, then fell down. The three men got up and ran to where the boy lay. Peters pulled a small dart[3] out of Michael's left arm and then helped Jeff to lift[4] the boy up. They carried him round the lake to Laird's Wood.

They had to find somewhere to hide until it got dark, and the wood was ideal[5]. They walked until they came to a small grassy space in the thickest part of the wood.

They lay Michael's unconscious[6] body on the ground and then sat down next to him.

'When do you think it'll be safe to leave, Slim?' asked Jeff.

'I think we'll have to wait until at least 9 o'clock,' said Wilson. 'It gets dark so late here in the north in the summer.'

'So we'll have to stay here for about six hours,' said Jeff.

'Yes,' replied Wilson. 'The boat's coming back to pick us up at 10 o'clock. How long does the effect[7] of the sleeping drug[8] last[9], Peters?'

'Twelve hours,' Peters answered.

'Good!' said Wilson. 'We'll just have to sit here and wait. Let's hope nobody starts looking for him.'

1 aim [em] (v.) 瞄準
2 fire [faɪr] (v.) 開槍
3 dart [dɑrt] (n.) 標槍

4 lift [lɪft] (v.) 舉起
5 ideal [aɪˋdiəl] (a.) 理想的
6 unconscious [ʌnˋkɑnʃəs] (a.) 不省人事的
7 effect [ɪˋfɛkt] (n.) 效果；作用
8 sleeping drug 安眠藥
9 last [læst] (v.) 持續

What happens next?

- What do you think happens next? Choose from the situations below.
  - a Michael wakes up before they leave and escapes from the three men.
  - b The three men kidnap[1] Michael and ask for a ransom[2] from George and Sarah.
  - c The three men want Michael to steal something for them.
  - d The three men want Michael to teach them to fly.
  - e One of the three men is Michael's real father and he wants to see him.
- Then continue the story for that situation.

Michael is missing

35 At ten to four Sarah started to get the tea ready. She made a pot[3] of tea and put some cakes on the table. Michael always came home hungry and thirsty after his afternoon walks. At four o'clock Dr Reed arrived to join them.

'It's a beautiful day, Sarah,' he said when she let him into the kitchen. 'One of the best we've had this summer.'

'Yes, it is,' said the Sarah. 'Sit down, Richard. Michael will be home soon. I'll go and call George. He's still working in the vegetable garden.'

'Well, actually, Sarah,' said the doctor. 'He's fast asleep in a garden chair in the sun.'

They both laughed as Sarah poured[4] the tea.

They drank tea, ate cakes and talked while they waited. At half past four Sarah stood up and went over to the window.

'It's not like Michael to be so late,' she said.

'Oh, don't worry, Sarah,' said Dr Reed. 'Where's he gone?'

'I don't know,' she answered. 'He had some homework to do.'

They waited for another fifteen minutes, then George came in.

'Hello, Richard,' he said. 'Is there any tea left, Sarah love?'

'Michael hasn't come back yet, George,' said Sarah.

1 kidnap [ˋkɪdnæp] (v.) 綁架
2 ransom [ˋrænsəm] (n.) 贖金
3 pot [pɑt] (n.) 壺
4 pour [por] (v.) 倒；灌

36 'Hasn't he?' answered her husband. 'I expect he's still watching the birds.'

'I'll just go and check his computer and find out what his homework was today,' said Dr Reed, and went upstairs. A few minutes later he came back into the kitchen.

'He's studying the plants[1] at the north end of Goose Loch,' he said. 'I'll walk up there and see what he's doing.'

It took Richard Reed twenty minutes to get to the lake. He looked all around and shouted 'Michael!' two or three times. But there was no answer. The doctor was puzzled. This was not like Michael. He was hardly ever[2] late for meals[3]. Tea was always at four o'clock. Now it was half past five.

'Did you hear that?' said Jeff.

'What?' asked Wilson, sitting up.

'Listen!' answered Jeff.

They heard a man's voice shouting, 'Michael!'

'That's the doctor,' said Jeff. 'Dr Reed.'

They sat very quietly and listened. The doctor called twice more.

Dr Reed went back to the house, hoping to find Michael there. But only Sarah and George were in the kitchen. Sarah began to cry.

1 plant [plænt] (n.) 植物
2 hardly ever 很少
3 meal [mil] (n.) 一餐
4 reliable [rɪ`laɪəbl̩] (a.) 可靠的
5 track [træk] (n.) 足跡
6 occasionally [ə`keʒənl̩ɪ] (adv.) 偶而
7 apart from 除了……之外

'Don't worry, love,' George said, putting his arm around her. 'He'll soon be home. He's probably found something interesting to do and has forgotten the time.'

But secretly he was worried too. Michael was always very reliable[4].

'I'm going to walk up to the top of Castle Hill,' said Dr Reed. 'I'll be able to see him from there. Can I borrow your binoculars, George?'

'Certainly!' he answered. 'Wait! I'll come with you.'

The two men set off along the track[5]. They walked quickly. It was now seven o'clock but it was still sunny and warm. Occasionally[6] one of them shouted 'Michael!', but apart from[7] that, neither of them said anything as they walked along.

The prisoner

38 When Michael woke up, he found himself in a small, dark place. He was inside a box and his hands were tied together behind his back. He knew that he must be in a car or a van[1] because he was thrown[2] to one side when the vehicle[3] went round a corner. For a moment he felt confused[4], but then his mind started to clear.

'I remember that I was studying flowers and suddenly I felt a pain in my arm. Then everything went dark. But where am I now? How did I get here? And where am I going?'

After what seemed like a long time, the car or van stopped and he heard voices.

'Help!' he shouted as loudly as he could. 'Help me!'

Slim Wilson looked at Jeff and Peters nervously.

'He's woken up,' said Wilson. 'Let's get him inside quickly.'

Peters unlocked the back doors of the van and together the three men lifted out a large box. There were several similar[5] boxes in the van.

'Let me out!' shouted Michael. But the three men took no notice.

They carried the box into a small room inside a building and put it on the floor.

'Now listen carefully, Michael,' said Wilson, putting his face very close to the box. 'We've got a job for you to do, and if you do it well, we'll let you go. But if you don't, we'll kill[2] Sarah Broad. She's here too, in another room here. Do you understand?'

'Yes,' said Michael. 'I understand. But let me out of here. I'm thirsty.'

Wilson made a sign[6] to Peters and Hunter. They opened the box, pulled Michael out and put him on a chair. When he saw the men, Michael felt really scared[7]. They were all wearing balaclavas[8] over their faces. One of them was holding a bottle of water.

'Please untie[9] my hands,' said Michael.

'Only if you promise to be good,' said Wilson. 'Remember what I said about Sarah.'

'I'll be good,' said Michael.

1 van [væn] (n.) 發財車
2 throw [θro] (v.) 丟；扔
3 vehicle [ˋviɪkḷ] (n.) 車輛
4 confused [kənˋfjuzd] (a.) 混亂的
5 similar [ˋsɪmələ˞] (a.) 相似的
6 sign [saɪn] (n.) 手勢
7 scared [skɛrd] (a.) 吃驚的；嚇壞的
8 balaclava [ˏbæləˋklɑvə] (n.) 只露出眼睛的覆頭絨帽
9 untie [ʌnˋtaɪ] (v.) 解開

40

Wilson nodded and Peters cut the rope[1]. Michael took the water and drank. Then, before Wilson knew what was happening, Michael threw the bottle at him, jumped up, opened his wings and flew up to the ceiling.

'Get him down!' shouted Wilson.

The three men tried to catch[2] the boy as he circled[3] the room. In the end Peters climbed onto the table, took hold of Michael's leg and pulled him down.

'If you do that again,' shouted Wilson angrily, 'Sarah will die! Tie his wings so that he can't fly!'

Peters and Hunter got some rope and tied it tightly[4] around Michael's wings and body.

'Now, listen!' said Wilson. 'I'll repeat what I said before. We want you to do a simple job for us, and then we'll let you go. We don't want to hurt you, and we don't want to hurt your mum. OK? If you do what we say, everything will be fine. Are you going to be a good boy?'

Michael nodded.

Michael

- How do you think Michael feels? Close your eyes and imagine you are Michael. Then describe how you feel. Think of the following.

  1 Where are you?
  2 Are you afraid?
  3 Have you got any pains?
  4 Who are the men?
  5 What are they going to ask you to do?

1 rope [rop] (n.) 繩子
2 catch [kætʃ] (v.) 抓住
3 circle [ˋsɝkḷ] (v.) 繞行
4 tightly [ˋtaɪtlɪ] (adv.) 緊緊地

41

Wilson looked at Jeff. 'Now give him some food before we tell him what he has to do.'

Jeff gave Michael some sandwiches. Jeff didn't speak, but Michael was sure that he knew this man. There was something familiar[1] about the way he moved. A little later, he took Michael into another room where there was a computer.

'Sit down, Michael, and watch this piece of film,' said Wilson.

Michael watched. He saw a high wall with guards[2] standing along it every few hundred meters. Then he saw the wall from the air. It surrounded a group of buildings. The camera zoomed in[3] on some of them – they looked like offices.

'Now, Michael,' said Wilson. 'Inside that building there is something that I want very much. And that's why I need your help. I want you to fly over the wall. And get something for me inside. Now come here and look at these plans[4].'

He took Michael to a large table in the corner where there were plans of the building.

'This is the building you have to go into,' said Wilson, pointing to a red square[5] on the first plan. 'And this is what it looks like inside.' He showed Michael a plan of a room. 'You have to go into this room, open this cupboard and take out an envelope with the word "Lion" written on the front.'

During the following two hours, Wilson gave Michael detailed instructions about what he had to do.

1 familiar [fəˋmɪljɚ] (a.) 熟悉的
2 guard [gɑrd] (n.) 守衛
3 zoom [zum] (v.) 將鏡頭推近或拉遠（zoom in，推近；zoom out 拉遠）
4 plan [plæn] (n.) 平面圖
5 square [skwɛr] (n.) 廣場
6 search [sɝtʃ] (v.) 搜尋
7 party [ˋpɑrtɪ] (n.) 一夥人

The search begins

42 Back on Shillan, the Broads and Dr Reed called the police. The police arrived by helicopter and started to search[6] the area. The following morning the search party[7] found footprints[8] on the sand at East Beach and the marks left by a rubber dinghy.

Just before midday, Detective[9] Riley went to the Broads' house to give them an up-to-date[10] report.

'So now we know he isn't on the island,' he said. 'And that he was taken away in a rubber dinghy.'

'Please find him soon!' sobbed[11] Sarah.

'We will, Mrs Broad. Don't worry!' said Riley gently. 'We have some of our best people working on it right now.'

'Have you got any ideas about who's kidnapped him?' asked George.

'A few,' Riley answered. 'The only people you've been in contact[12] with are the four from the BBC. We've already spoken to three of them, but we can't find Hunter.'

'Jeff?' asked Dr Reed.

'Yes, the technician,' said the detective.

'So what can we do?' asked George.

'Nothing at the moment, I'm afraid,' replied Riley. 'But if it's any comfort to you, we're giving this case top priority[13].'

8 footprint [ˋfʊt͵prɪnt] (n.) 腳印
9 detective [dɪˋtɛktɪv] (n.) 偵探
10 up-to-date [ˋʌptəˋdet] (a.) 包含最新訊息的
11 sob [sɑb] (v.) 嗚咽；啜泣
12 contact [ˋkɑntækt] (n.) 聯絡
13 priority [praɪˋɔrətɪ] (n.) 優先

Breaking In

43

The next morning, Peters dyed[1] Michael's beautiful white feathers black.

'To make you more difficult to see at night!'

While they dried, Wilson put a belt around Michael's waist and fitted[2] two electronic[3] gadgets[4] to it. One was a transmitter[5] he could use to talk to Wilson. The other was an explosive[6] device[7].

'If you do anything wrong, Michael, this device will explode[8] and that will be the end of you! And the end of Sarah Broad!' Wilson said. Then he gave Michael a microphone and headphones[9] to use with the transmitter. Wilson told him to practice talking to Peters in the next room so that they could check the system.

Around three o'clock, Michael had to put on a black jacket, black trousers and a black balaclava. He was now certain that one of the men was Jeff from the BBC, even though he never spoke and the others never used his name.

At five o'clock, the gang[10], with Michael, set off[11] for the Government Nuclear[12] Research Complex[13]. They made Michael get back into the box and then put the box back into the van. Michael's wings were still tied and he was very uncomfortable. They drove for about four hours and he was very happy when the van finally stopped and the men let him out.

1 dye [daɪ] (v.) 染色 (n.) 染色；染料
2 fit [fɪt] (v.) 安裝
3 electronic [ˌɪlɛkˋtrɑnɪk] (a.) 電子操縱的
4 gadget [ˋɡædʒɪt] (n.) 小機件；儀器
5 transmitter [trænsˋmɪtɚ] (n.) 發送器
6 explosive [ɪkˋsplosɪv] (a.) 爆炸性的

'There's the complex,' said Wilson, pointing to a wall with some floodlights[14] on the top. 'Now, Michael! You know what you have to do, and you know what will happen if you do anything different, don't you?'

'Yes,' said Michael. 'I know.' He was scared but he didn't show it. He didn't want to help these criminals[15] steal secret documents[16] from this government building. And he didn't want to be discovered and shot by the guards.

'Good,' said Wilson. 'OK, you two! Untie his wings!'

When Hunter and Peters took off the rope, Michael opened and closed his wings a few times. Wilson checked his watch.

'Right, a quarter to ten,' he said. 'We have fifteen minutes before they change the guards and you go in, Michael. Let's check the electrical equipment.'

Jeff came and switched on the various gadgets attached[17] to Michael's belt, and then he checked Wilson and Peters' monitors[18]. They all tested their microphones and headphones to see if they were working correctly.

'Thanks, Jeff,' said Michael quietly when Peters and Wilson were talking together a few meters away.

'That's OK . . . Huh? What did you say?' asked Hunter with a surprised look on his face

'I said, "Thanks, Jeff",' replied Michael.

7 device [dɪ`vaɪs] (n.) 裝置
8 explode [ɪk`splod] (v.) 爆炸
9 headphone [`hɛd,fon] (n.) 頭戴式耳機
10 gang [gæŋ] (n.)（歹徒等的）一幫
11 set off 動身；出發
12 nuclear [`njuklɪɚ] (a.) 核子能的
13 complex [`kɑmplɛks] (n.) 綜合設施
14 floodlight [`flʌd,laɪt] (n.) 泛光燈
15 criminal [`krɪmən!] (n.) 罪犯
16 document [`dɑkjəmənt] (n.) 文件
17 attach [ə`tætʃ] (v.) 裝上；繫上
18 monitor [`mɑnətɚ] (n.) 監聽器；監視器

'How did you . . . er . . . My name isn't Jeff. It's . . . er . . . it's . . . Steve,' replied Hunter, not very convincingly[1].

'Oh, sorry – Steve!' said Michael. 'You remind[2] me of someone I know.'

'Are we ready, then?' asked Wilson, walking over to Michael and Hunter.

'Yes. Everything's working perfectly,' answered Jeff.

'Good,' said Wilson. 'It's time to go then, Michael.'

Michael took off and flew high into the sky. He flew in large circles above the three men. Up, up, up! Soon he was above the beams[3] of the floodlights. As he hovered[4] in the air, he thought about landing in the courtyard and telling the guards the truth. 'A gang of criminals has kidnapped me and they want me to steal something very important from here. Help me, please!'

But no, he couldn't do that. The criminals were following all his moves[5] on their transmitters. So, what could he do? He thought and thought but he didn't have an answer to that question. He decided to wait and see[6] what happened inside the building.

1 convincingly [kən`vɪnsɪŋlɪ] (adv.) 令人信服地
2 remind [rɪ`maɪnd] (v.) 提醒
3 beam [bim] (n.) 光束
4 hover [`hʌvɚ] (v.) 盤旋
5 move [muv] (n.) 動作
6 wait and see 觀望

The police get closer

'Any news?' asked George as Riley came back into the living room after a long phone conversation. It was four o'clock in the afternoon. Hundreds of miles away, the criminals were getting ready to set off for the Nuclear Complex.

'Yes, there is,' said the detective. 'Our people have searched Hunter's flat[1] and checked his emails. In his emails he talks about an "objective[2]" in the north of England. He also adds[3] that it is "remote[4]". We think that the people who have taken Michael want to use him to fly into a place which is surrounded by a high wall or something similar. We have found four places like this in the north of England and we're sending officers to each of those now. We have also located[5] the house of the person that Hunter was emailing.'

'But there's no news of Michael?' asked Sarah.

'I'm afraid not,' answered Riley. 'But we're getting closer every minute.'

Just then, Riley's mobile phone[6] rang. 'Excuse me,' he said and he went outside. Five minutes later he came back in with a strange expression on his face.

'Good news?' asked George. 'Or bad news?'

'Well both, actually,' replied Riley. 'Hunter was emailing a man called Edward Wilson, known as "Slim". That's the good news because now we know who we're looking for.'

'And the bad news?' asked George.

1 flat [flæt] (n.)〔英〕公寓
2 objective [əb`dʒɛktɪv] (n.) 目標
3 add [æd] (v.) 補充說
4 remote [rɪ`mot] (a.) 遙遠的
5 locate [lo`ket] (v.) 座落於
6 mobile phone〔英〕手機

'Wilson is a well-known international criminal. We've examined his computer and discovered that he is working with an important terrorist[7] group. The "objective" in the north of England is something that the terrorists want. And they'll pay a lot of money for it.'

'Oh dear,' said George. 'And Michael is involved[8] too, now.'

'Yes,' said Riley. 'However, it makes the possible site easier to identify[9]. We think they're going to break into[10] either the Warefield Military Weapons[11] Establishment[12] near York or the Government Nuclear Research Complex outside Leeds. So we're sending most of our men to those two sites. The employees[13] at both places have been told to continue working normally so that the criminals don't become suspicious[14]. We need to catch Wilson and stop him from selling any more government secrets to terrorist groups.'

'But what about Michael?' asked Sarah tearfully[15].

'He'll be alright, Mrs Broad,' said Riley kindly. 'We'll make sure of that!'

Email

- Do you use email? Have you got your own email address? Who do you send emails to? Which of the following do you use? Tick (✓).

  ☐ A social network ☐ A photo-sharing network
  ☐ A chat program ☐ A music-sharing network
  ☐ A blog
- Share the results in class.

7 terrorist [ˋtɛrərɪst] (n.) 恐怖分子
8 involved [ɪnˋvɑlvd] (a.) 牽扯在內的
9 identify [aɪˋdɛntəˏfaɪ] (v.) 確認；識別
10 break into 闖入
11 weapon [ˋwɛpən] (n.) 武器
12 establishment [ɪsˋtæblɪʃmənt] (n.) 機構
13 employee [ˏɛmplɔɪˋi] (n.) 員工
14 suspicious [səˋspɪʃəs] (a.) 猜疑的
15 tearfully [ˋtɪrfəlɪ] (adv.) 含淚地

Michael flies in

48 When he was high enough, Michael looked down. He could see the van parked among the trees, but he couldn't see the gang. He started to fly towards the wall. He went through the details of the plan in his head. He had to wait until he heard the bell ring at ten o'clock. It took fifteen minutes for the guards to change. During those fifteen minutes there was nobody outside the building. That was when he had to fly in.

He dropped a little lower in the sky and hovered there, waiting. A minute later the bell rang and he saw the guards start to move away from their posts[1]. He flew quickly over the wall and dropped down to the ground next to the building he had to enter[2]. There was a sign[3] saying 'Head Office[4]' on it. He spoke quietly into his microphone.

'I'm outside the building.'

'Right.' (*Wilson's voice.*) 'Walk round to the main[5] door.'

The lights were very bright in the courtyard. Michael was shaking all over. 'Someone's sure to see me,' he thought.

'I'm at the main door.'

'OK. Now press[6] these keys on the number pad[7] on the door. Ready? 7-8-5-0-7-9-9.

'OK. Done.'

1 post [post] (n.) 位置
2 enter [ˋɛntɚ] (v.) 進入
3 sign [saɪn] (n.) 招牌
4 head office 總部
5 main [men] (a.) 主要的
6 press [prɛs] (v.) 按壓
7 number pad 數字鍵盤

MICHAEL, DON
SPEAK!
THE POLICE ARE
HERE YOU
WALK TO THE
OFFICE THE
ALARMS ARE OFF

49 'Now press the key that says "Enter".'

Michael pressed the 'Enter' key. He heard a click[1].

'The door's open.'

'Good. Now go and do everything I told you to do. Call me again when you get out with the "Lion" envelope.'

Michael knew that, once inside, he had to fly up to the ceiling of the corridor[2] in front of him. The office he had to go to was at the end of this corridor. He had to fly because there were electronic sensors[3] connected to the alarm system[4] in the lower part of the walls of the corridor.

He slowly pushed the door open. To his amazement[5], he saw a man in military uniform standing in the middle of the corridor. He was holding a large sign which said:

MICHAEL, DON'T SPEAK!
ITS OK.
THE POLICE ARE HERE.
YOU CAN WALK TO THE OFFICE.
THE ALARMS ARE OFF[6].

1 click [klɪk] (n.) 卡嗒聲
2 corridor [ˋkɔrɪdɚ] (n.) 走廊
3 sensor [ˋsɛnsɚ] (n.) 感應器
4 alarm system 警報系統
5 amazement [əˋmezmənt] (n.) 吃驚
6 off [ɔf] (a.)（電器等）關著的
7 tracking device 追蹤器
8 cheerily [ˋtʃɪrɪlɪ] (adv.) 興高采烈地
9 thumbs up sign 大拇指向上的手勢

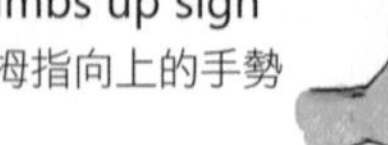

10 flap [flæp] (v.) 拍打

The man smiled, and Michael smiled back. He walked down the corridor to the office, where there was a uniformed policeman. He held a sign which said:

MICHAEL, DON'T SAY ANYTHING!
TAKE THE ENVELOPE OUT OF THE CUPBOARD.
THERE'S A TRACKING DEVICE[7] IN IT.
THERE'S ANOTHER TRACKING DEVICE
ON THE DESK.
PUT IT IN YOUR POCKET.

Michael found the envelope and put it in his pocket, together with the tracking device. He waved cheerily[8] at the policeman and walked out of the office and down the corridor. For the first time in two days, he didn't feel so frightened. As he stepped out into the courtyard, two more policemen smiled and gave him the thumbs up sign[9]. He spoke into his microphone, 'I've got the "Lion" envelope.'

'Good!' said Wilson. 'Now fly straight back to us.'

He flapped[10] his wings and flew up high to get above the lights. He knew that he had to follow the plan so as not to make the men suspicious. As he flew over the wall, he started to feel scared again.

Good news on Shillan

51 'We've found him!' said Detective Riley to the Broads as he came back into the living room after his latest phone call.

'Oh, that's wonderful news!' said Sarah. 'Where is he now?'

'He's still with the criminals,' answered Riley. 'But our officers have given him a tracking device so we can follow him everywhere he goes.'

'But why is he back with the criminals?' asked Sarah. 'Isn't that dangerous?'

'We need to catch these people, Mrs Broad,' said Detective Riley, 'And we think that they will lead us to the terrorists. We can't rescue[1] Michael yet. We need him.'

'Oh, dear!' said Sarah. 'So he's not safe at all. You're going to use him to find those terrible people.'

'I'm sorry, Mrs Broad,' answered Riley. 'But you must understand that I'm doing this for the safety of the country, and perhaps the whole world. We have to catch these people now.'

Detective Riley

- Do you think Detective Riley did the correct thing? What does Sarah think?
- Imagine you are Detective Riley. Explain your plans to a partner.

The appointment

Michael flew back to where the three men were hiding.

'Here it is!' he said, handing over the "Lion" envelope.

'Good boy!' said Wilson, smiling. 'You've done a great job.' Then he turned to Peters and Hunter. 'And now, gentlemen! Let's go and meet our friends!'

'What about the boy?' asked Peters.

'We'll take him with us, just in case[2],' replied Wilson. 'Tie him up!' said Wilson. 'And take off the belt, microphone and headphones, too! Then put him back in the box. I'm not taking any chances.

The whole country's probably looking for him now. And change into your normal clothes as soon as you've put him into the van.'

Jeff Hunter dug[3] a hole in the ground and buried[4] their black clothes and balaclavas. Then they got in the van.

'Where to, Slim?' asked Peters, who was driving.

'Drive south!' answered Wilson. 'Follow the signs for the M62 motorway[5], then go west. We're heading for Manchester Airport. I have an appointment[6] with our clients[7] at six o'clock tomorrow morning so we've got plenty of[8] time. Drive slowly and carefully. I'm going to have a little sleep now. Wake me up when we're ten miles from the airport.'

1 rescue [ˋrɛskju] (v.) 營救
2 in case 假使
3 dig [dɪg] (v.) 挖掘
4 bury [ˋbɛrɪ] (v.) 埋葬
5 motorway [ˋmotɚ͵we] (n.)〔英〕高速公路
6 appointment [əˋpɔɪntmənt] (n.) 正式約會
7 client [ˋklaɪənt] (n.) 委託人；客戶
8 plenty of 很多；大量

53 They got to the motorway just after midnight. Wilson was still asleep. Hunter was staring[1] out of the window. He was worried. Did Michael really know who he was? Peters was thinking about his share of the payment[2] – a million pounds[3]! Neither of them noticed that two dark blue cars were following them. They didn't hear the helicopter flying above them either.

When they were ten miles from the airport, Peters said: 'Wake up, Slim! We're nearly there.'

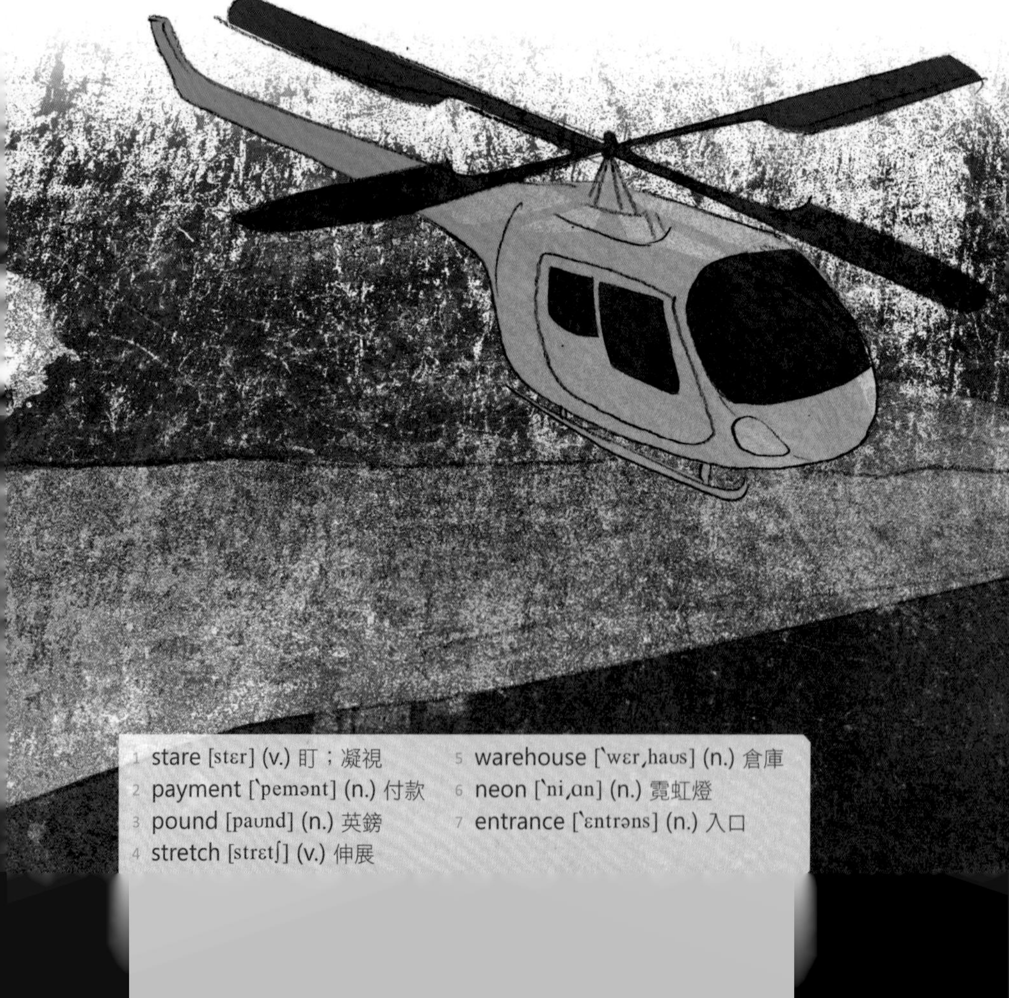

1 stare [stɛr] (v.) 盯；凝視
2 payment [ˋpemənt] (n.) 付款
3 pound [paʊnd] (n.) 英鎊
4 stretch [strɛtʃ] (v.) 伸展
5 warehouse [ˋwɛr͵haʊs] (n.) 倉庫
6 neon [ˋni͵ɑn] (n.) 霓虹燈
7 entrance [ˋɛntrəns] (n.) 入口

Wilson yawned and stretched[4]. He looked at the road signs on the motorway. 'OK, Peters,' he said. 'We're not actually going to the airport. I'm meeting my clients at the Grand Hotel. You'll see a sign for it soon.'

About three miles from the airport, they turned off and drove through an area with hotels, car parks and warehouses[5].

'There it is!' said Hunter, pointing to a large square building with the name 'Grand Hotel' in bright neon[6] lights on the roof.

'Right,' said Wilson. 'Drive into the car park, Peters, and find somewhere quiet to park. Not too far away. I want to be able to see the entrance[7].'

54

Peters parked and Slim Wilson looked at his watch. 'Good,' he said. 'Almost three o'clock. I booked[1] a room here last week so I'll just go up and have a shower and make myself smart[2] before my clients arrive. You two can stay in the van. But keep your eyes open. Peters, get your gun ready just in case something goes wrong[3]. We'll meet again when I've done the deal[4].'

He took his briefcase[5] containing[6] the "Lion" envelope and walked across the car park and through the glass doors of the hotel.

At the same time as Wilson went to have his shower, two dark blue cars entered the hotel car park. One of them parked opposite[7] the entrance and the other one parked opposite the van.

At five o'clock, while Peters and Hunter were dozing[8] in their van, a large white van with 'Conference[9] Logistics[10]' written on its side parked immediately outside the hotel entrance. A lot of men dressed in white overalls[11] climbed out and opened the back doors. They unloaded[12] lots of boards[13] and signs and other equipment and carried everything into the lobby[14] of the hotel.

'What's going on?' asked Peters, waking up suddenly.

Hunter yawned. 'Oh, it looks like there's a conference at the hotel today,' he said. 'Look at the banner[15] that they're putting up above the entrance. It says *3rd National Conference: Surgery*[16] *Today*. It must be an event[17] for doctors. They often have them at these hotels.'

1 book [buk] (v.) 預訂
2 smart [smɑrt] (a.) 漂亮的；時髦的
3 go wrong 出差錯
4 deal [dil] (n.) 交易
5 briefcase [ˋbrif͵kes] (n.) 公事包
6 contain [kənˋten] (v.) 包含
7 opposite [ˋɑpəzɪt] (prep.) 對面的
8 doze [doz] (v.) 打瞌睡

The men in the van

- Who do you think the men in the white van are? Tick (✓).
  - ☐ They are helpers at the conference.
  - ☐ They are policemen.
  - ☐ They are terrorists.
- What happens next?

55

'Well, I hope they move that van soon – we can't see what's going on.' said Peters.

The two men watched as the workers continued to unload the van. At a quarter to six, it was driven away and parked behind the hotel.

'Fifteen minutes to go,' said Peters. 'Oh, look! There's Wilson.'

Hunter saw Slim Wilson standing at the hotel entrance, looking out over the car park. He was dressed in a very smart suit and he was holding his briefcase. Suddenly, he went back inside and said something to the receptionist[18]. Then he went and sat down on a sofa.

'He's waiting for the contact to arrive,' said Peters. 'With our lovely money!'

9 conference [ˋkɑnfərəns] (n.) 會議
10 logistics [loˋdʒɪstɪks] (n.) 後勤；運籌
11 overall [ˋovɚ,ɔl] (n.)〔英〕工作服
12 unload [ʌnˋlod] (v.) 卸貨
13 board [bord] (n.) 牌子
14 lobby [ˋlɑbɪ] (n.) 大廳
15 banner [ˋbænɚ] (n.) 旗幟
16 surgery [ˋsɝdʒərɪ] (n.) 外科
17 event [ɪˋvɛnt] (n.) 活動
18 receptionist [rɪˋsɛpʃənɪst] (n.) 接待員

56

'Yeah!' said Hunter. 'I've got a ticket to the States[1] in my pocket. I'm catching a plane from here at eleven o'clock and then a flight to New York from Heathrow[2] at four this afternoon. Bye-bye Britain! Hello new life of luxury[3]!'

The two men laughed. They watched as a lot of cars and vans drove into the car park and filled up[4] most of the available[5] spaces. Men in dark suits got out and walked over to the hotel entrance.

'It's busy here this morning, isn't it?' remarked[6] Peters. 'I don't like it. Too many people.'

'Don't worry, Peters!' said Hunter. 'It's just people arriving for the conference.'

1 the States 指美國
2 Heathrow [`hiθro] (n.) 希斯洛機場（倫敦的機場）
3 luxury [`lʌkʃərɪ] (n.) 奢侈；奢華
4 fill up 填滿
5 available [ə`veləbḷ] (a.) 有空的
6 remark [rɪ`mɑrk] (v.) 談論；説
7 endgame [`ɛndgem] (n.) 尾聲
8 unmarked [ʌn`mɑrkt] (a.) 無記號的
9 pull into（車子）開進
10 pretend [prɪ`tɛnd] (v.) 假裝
11 organizer [`ɔrgə,naɪzɚ] (n.) 組織幹部

Endgame[7]

57 Nobody noticed the police helicopter land at Manchester Airport at five thirty that morning. Nobody saw Detective Riley and George and Sarah Broad get out of it and get into a blue unmarked[8] police car that was waiting for them.

When the car pulled into[9] the Grand Hotel car park and parked a little while later, Detective Riley explained what was happening. 'Can you see those men in white overalls? They're our people. They're pretending[10] to be conference organizers[11]. Michael is in the white computer van over there on the right, and two of the criminals are with him. Wilson is waiting inside to meet the person who he's going to sell the nuclear secrets to.'

58 'I didn't know airport hotels were so busy at this time in the morning. Look at all those people!'

Riley smiled. 'They're police officers too, Mrs Broad. They're pretending to be doctors arriving for the conference. The plan is that all our men will fill the reception area so that Wilson and his client can't get away.'

'It's just like in one of those TV thrillers[1],' said George, smiling.

At one minute to six a black limousine[2] stopped outside the hotel. A very elegantly[3] dressed gentleman carrying a suitcase[4] got out. He went into the reception area of the hotel and spoke to the receptionist, who pointed to the sofa where Slim Wilson was sitting. Wilson stood up, smiled, and the two men shook hands. Then they sat down and started talking.

A minute or two later, Wilson took the Lion envelope out of his briefcase and handed it to the other man, who put his suitcase on the coffee table in front of them. They shook hands again. Then, twenty or thirty men, some in suits, some in overalls, suddenly seemed to appear from nowhere. They quickly surrounded Wilson and the other man, who had no chance of running away. They were handcuffed[5] and taken to a room at the back of the hotel.

At the same moment, more officers surrounded the limousine in the car park. Others pulled open the doors of the computer van where Hunter and Peters were sitting, speechless[6] with surprise. They led the two men away to one of the blue vans waiting in the car park.

1 thriller [ˋθrɪlɚ] (n.) 驚悚片
2 limousine [ˋlɪmə͵zin] (n.) 豪華轎車
3 elegantly [ˋɛləgəntlɪ] (adv.) 講究地
4 suitcase [ˋsut͵kes] (n.) 手提箱
5 handcuff [ˋhænd͵kʌf] (v.) 戴上手銬
6 speechless [ˋspitʃlɪs] (a.) 一時說不出話來的

59 Riley and the Broads immediately ran to the computer van. The detective found the key and opened the back door.

'Michael,' he shouted. 'Michael, where are you?'

'In here,' came a muffled[1] voice from inside the box.

Two policemen carefully lifted the box out, laid it on the ground and opened it. The morning sun shone directly into Michael's eyes and he blinked[2]. For a few minutes he couldn't see all the people standing around him, smiling.

'Michael!' Sarah was the first person to speak. 'Michael!' She hugged him tightly to her chest. Then George hugged both of them.

'Are you all right?' asked George.

'Yes, I'm fine,' said Michael, with a big smile on his face. 'But could someone untie my wings, please?'

'Oh, Michael! What happened to your lovely white feathers?' cried Sarah.

'Don't worry, Sarah! It's only dye. It'll soon wash out[3],' replied Michael, putting his arm around her.

Michael and the Broads didn't go back to Shillan immediately. They stayed in a luxurious suite[4] in the best hotel in Manchester for a week because the police needed to question[5] the boy. While they were there, they watched the episode of *Strange But True* about Michael on TV. The last two days of the week were filled with[6] discussions about Michael's future. There were many decisions to make.

When the Broads, Michael and Dr Reed flew back to Shillan, two policemen went with them They were Michael's permanent[7] bodyguards[8], so Michael was able to spend the rest of the summer relaxing and enjoying himself. Then the end of August arrived and it was time to move again.

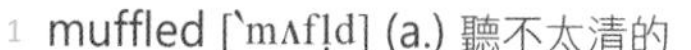

1 muffled [ˋmʌfḷd] (a.) 聽不太清的
2 blink [blɪŋk] (v.) 閃爍
3 wash out 褪掉
4 suite [swit] (n.) 套房
5 question [ˋkwɛstʃən] (v.) 訊問
6 fill with 充滿
7 permanent [ˋpɝmənənt] (a.) 永久的
8 bodyguard [ˋbadɪˏgard] (n.) 保鏢

Epilogue[1]

60

In early September the Broads and Michael moved to a village in the north of England and Michael joined the third year at the local secondary school[2]. People accepted him without asking too many questions and he soon made lots of friends. Then, when he was eighteen, things changed. George died and Michael went to university to study Biology. He got a good degree[3] and went on to do an MSc[4]. His thesis[5] was on the rare flowers of Shillan.

Then he returned to the village and lived with Sarah. When she died he got a job teaching Biology at his secondary school. His students always enjoyed his lessons on flight the most because he took them out onto the sports fields[6] for real live[7] demonstrations[8].

He flew for his own pleasure about once a week, but always when nobody was around to watch him.

Dr Reed kept in touch and visited him once every three months to record details of any changes. Now we must leave the man who could fly where we found him – crossing the park on his way home to have his supper.

1 epilogue [ˋɛpə͵lɔg] (n.) 結尾；尾聲
2 secondary school 中學
3 degree [dɪˋgri] (n.) 學位
4 MSc 理工科碩士學位（Masters in Science）
5 thesis [ˋθisɪs] (n.) 學位論文
6 sports field 體育場
7 live [laɪv] (a.) 實況播送的
8 demonstration [͵dɛmənˋstreʃən] (n.) 示範

AFTER READING

A Personal Response

1. What did you think of this story? Write a paragraph describing your reaction to it.

2. Write a 150-word summary of the story.

3. Which character did you like most, and which least? Why?

4. Which part of the story did you like best? Explain why.

5. Is there anything in the story that you would have liked to change? Can you think of any way to improve the story?

6. Does the story remind you of any other books you have read or films or TV series you've watched? If so, which ones, and why?

B Comprehension

7 Explain who these people are, what they do and how they are connected to Michael. Write one sentence about each of them.

a) George and Sarah Broad — They are the couple who find Michael and adopt him as their son.

b) Jeff Hunter

c) Richard Reed

d) Paul Salter

e) Slim Wilson

f) Detective Riley

8 Explain why the doctors keep Michael at the hospital. Does Michael like being there?

9 Do you think it was right or wrong for Michael to escape from the hospital? Discuss your reasons with a partner.

10 What happens after Michael escapes from the hospital? Describe the situation he finds at home.

11 Describe Michael's life on Shillan before he is kidnapped. Would you like to live like that? What are the advantages and disadvantages? Share in groups.

12 How did Wilson and his gang discover where Michael lived? Why was it important that Hunter remembered Michael's exact words to him?

13 What did Wilson want Michael to get for him? What is Wilson going to do with it when he gets it?

14 Who is inside the high-security building when Michael opens the door? What are they holding? Why? Use the same method to give a partner instructions.

15 Where does Wilson go after he gets the envelope? Who does he meet and why?

16 How are the police able to follow Wilson's gang and Michael?

17 How do the police manage to capture the criminals? Describe what happens at the hotel and how the police trick the criminals.

18 Do you think that Michael is happy at the end of the book?

C Characters

19 Answer these questions about the names of people in the story:

a) Why does Sarah call the baby she finds Michael?

b) What is 'Slim' Wilson's real name?

c) What is the newsagent's name?

d) Who is Mary?

e) What do you know about Mr Smith?

f) Who is the 'big man' who does exercises with Michael?

g) Who are Sally Roberts and Paul Brown?

20 Which of the people in Exercise **19** above are important in the story, and why? Which ones are not important to the story?

21 In different parts of the story, Michael is happy and unhappy. Give examples from the story and explain why he feels the way he does.

22 Who says the following things? When do they say them and who do they say them to?

a) Why do I have to be here? I'm sick of living in a hospital.

b) What you did was very wrong. We told you Michael couldn't go home.

c) I've had a phone call from my boss in London. The BBC have asked if they can make a film about Michael.

d) Hey, Mickey! What are you doing?

e) It's busy here this morning, isn't it? I don't like it. Too many people.

f) Oh, Michael! What happened to your lovely white feathers?

23 Choose one of these characters and write a description of them.

Dr Richard Reed   Jeff Hunter   Slim Wilson   Detective Riley

24 What is Michael like at the beginning and end of the story (when he is an adult)? What is his life like? Do you think he's happy? Why/why not?

D Plot and theme

25 Look at these four pictures and write the order in which they happen.

26 Now write a sentence about what is happening in each of them.

27 Who tells this story?

- (a) Michael
- (b) An external narrator
- (c) Another character from the story

Find examples from the story to explain your choice.

28 How are the first and last chapters different from the others? What is the effect of this? Is it a good idea? Why/why not?

29 What are the main events in the story? Write them below.

The Broads find Michael on their doorstep

....

....

....

....

....

....

The police find Michael at the Grand Hotel, Manchester

30 What is the most exciting part of the story? Why?

31 Do you think the story has a happy ending? If so, what makes it happy? If not, why not?

32 What do you think about the way Michael is treated by the doctors and the police?

33 What are the main themes of the story? Choose two below and in groups find examples. Think of examples of them in real life.

a Difference
b Crime doesn't pay
c Media
d Integration
e Institutions
f Trust
g Town life versus life in isolation

E Language

34 Unscramble these words connected to flying. Write if the words are the nouns or verbs.

a ria ______
b ratfehe ______
c revoh ______
d giwn ______
e tgifhl ______
f lyf ______

35 Put the verbs in the box into the simple past then write them in the correct spaces.

fly hover land open rise

a Michael ______ in circles above the park.
b Michael moved his wings and slowly ______ into the air.
c Michael ______ his lovely white wings.
d Michael ______ in the same place without moving.
e Michael was getting dizzy, so he ______ in the park.

36 Write the words in the correct order to make sentences.

a on / family / Shillan / to / the / live / moved
The family moved to live on Shillan.

b every / Dr Reed / Michael / day / exercises / filmed / doing / his

c Biology / was / Michael / very / in / interested

d discovered / Wilson's / police / was / gang / where / the

e take / Michael / envelope / Wilson / to / an / wanted

f clothes / Michael / made / for / special / Sarah

37 Write one of the adjectives in the box into the correct sentence.

happy	frightened	worried	beautiful	rare

a Michael, Sarah and George were very ________ when they moved to Shillan.
b Michael grew ________ white feathers on his wings.
c Michael studied the ________ flowers of Shillan for his Biology project.
d Sarah was very ________ when Michael didn't come home for tea.
e Michael was ________ when Wilson told him what he had to do.

38 Complete the sentences with adverbs. Use the adjectives in brackets.

a *Slowly*, Michael found that he could move his wings. (slow)
b Michael moved his wings ________ backwards and forwards. (gentle)
c The three men walked ________ down Castle Hill towards Michael. (silent)
d The Broads ________ told the police about finding the baby. (immediate)
e Michael was surprised when he ________ rose in the air for the first time. (sudden)
f Jeff was ________ trying to be friendly to Michael. (obvious)

39 Make questions and answers in the past simple.

a what / Sarah / do / on Shillan / ?
b when / Michael / grow / wings / ?
c how / Michael / escape / from hospital / ?
d what / want / Wilson / steal / Michael / to / ?
e who / discover / where / Michael / live / ?

40 Now ask and answer the questions in Exercise **39** with a partner.

TEST

1 Read this description of Michael Broad's life as an adult, and choose the most suitable word for each space.

At university, Michael studied Biology, and after Sarah died, he got a job teaching the (a) ________ at his old secondary school. He was very (b) ________ in flowers, and wrote many articles on the wild plants of the north of England. He often went away at the weekend to places in the hills and valleys to (c) ________ wild flowers and photograph them. Sometimes, to save time, he (d) ________ around. This was a good way of (e) ________ time—he was able to fly to the top of a hill in about five minutes, when a walk took him over an hour. Of course, he (f) ________ seeing all the flowers on the way up when he flew, so he usually walked. At school Michael was a very (g) ________ teacher, and the students loved it when he taught them about flight. Then he took the students outside and (h) ________ them the things he told them about in class.

a	① object	② material	③ subject
b	① interesting	② interest	③ interested
c	① study	② watch	③ look
d	① flow	② flew	③ flied
e	① save	② to save	③ saving
f	① hadn't	② didn't	③ wasn't
g	① popular	② like	③ friend
h	① watched	② saw	③ showed

2 Imagine you are Michael. You are in the hotel in Manchester. The police want you to write down what happened to you when you were with Slim Wilson's gang. Write about everything from when they shot you on Shillan until when the police set you free at the Grand Hotel in Manchester. Use your own words.

3 Read the sentences. Then tick (✓).

- T F ⓐ George and Sarah Broad are Michael's natural parents.
- T F ⓑ When Michael is 12 years old, he grows wings.
- T F ⓒ Michael lives in a hospital for a long time.
- T F ⓓ The newspaper and TV reporters help Michael escape from hospital.
- T F ⓔ Michael, Sarah and George go and live on a farm in the north of England.
- T F ⓕ The cameraman from the BBC is also a criminal.
- T F ⓖ The gang use Michael because he can fly into a building they can't enter.
- T F ⓗ The police catch the gang at the Nuclear Complex near Leeds.

4 Look at the picture (page 85) and ask a partner questions about what you can see in it.

Flight

In groups make a poster, or a booklet or a presentation on ONE of the following.

a) How birds fly

Find out about:

1. the physical features that birds have (e.g. wings, feathers, muscles, bones)
2. how they move their wings when they fly
3. different ways of flying
4. how fast and how far birds can fly

Leonardo Da Vinci's drawings and experiments

ⓑ The history of human flight

Find out about:

1 early attempts, and stories (e.g. Icarus)

2 Leonardo Da Vinci's drawings and experiments

3 the first balloons (e.g. the Montgolfier brothers)

4 the first powered flight (e.g. the Wright brothers)

5 the development of jet engines

6 supersonic flight (e.g. Concorde)

作者簡介

大衛，你好！能跟我們介紹一下你自己嗎？

好啊！我是英國渥莎地方的人，學校畢業後受訓成為教師，在英格蘭任教。1977 年，我離開英國，旅居過義大利、塞爾維亞和匈牙利，也曾在其他三十個國家與世界各地的學子和教師共事過。最近，我把時間投入在編寫教材，包括文學創作和文學改寫，就像這本書一樣；此外我也負責指導英文教師。工作之餘，我會在一個藍調樂團裡擔任演奏，並研究大自然、藝術和建築。此外我還大量閱讀並創作短篇小說和詩歌。

本篇故事的創作靈感是怎麼來的？

我一直就對鳥類情有獨鐘，特別著迷於牠們美麗的翱翔。賞鳥，是我最早就培養出來的興趣之一。我老是想，我要是也能飛，那該有多好呀！故事的靈感首先來自於這個想法：人要是也有一對翅膀，飛翔起來將會是怎樣的一番情境？然後我又想到一個人如果會飛，可能會遇到哪些問題。

這則故事想要傳達的是什麼？

這則故事想要傳達的是，人類應該要能包容各種差異性，而且人們應該對有所差異的事物感到愉悅才是。正因為有所不同，我們的世界才顯得有趣。同樣重要的是，我們人類自身也是各有差異的，我們應該互相接納、擁抱，尊重彼此的個體性。

現在

P. 13

離地表一百公尺的空中，會飛翔的男子輕輕地前後揮動他的白色大翅膀。

在這種高度的上空，非常安靜，空氣乾淨又清新。他低頭俯瞰，看見自己居住的村莊和任教的學校，轉過頭來看得到公園和更遠處點綴著乳牛和綿羊的田野。

他稍稍加快揮動翅膀的速度，飛得更高些，更多景色映入眼簾：遠方那些丘陵是貝拉克山，藍色大大的那一大塊是威特利湖。

這時，他開始覺得有點頭暈噁心。在這個高度飛翔，對他來說是輕而易舉的，但是俯瞰下方遙遠的地面，總讓他覺得詭異。他有時候擔心自己會掉下來，當然，這事還沒發生過。鳥類不會摔落地面，而他就像一隻鳥。

他望著鄉間景色看了最後一眼，然後大幅地張開翅膀，緩緩盤旋了幾圈後，優雅地飛向下方的公園。

他用雙腳輕鬆降落地面。他把翅膀收折平貼背部，然後穿上那件特大號的特製外套遮蓋翅膀，現在看起來就跟平常人沒有兩樣。他穿越草坪走回家，開始琢磨著晚餐要吃什麼。

飛翔過後總讓他胃口大開。

話說從頭

P. 14

沒有人知道麥可的身世。一家小店鋪的老闆莎拉．布洛德和喬治．布洛德夫婦，他們某日清晨在自家門階上發現了麥可。當時他躺在一個籃子裡，籃內還有一袋新衣和一些嬰兒用品。莎拉推測他當時只有九個月大，後來她在袋子裡發現一張紙，上頭寫著「麥可」這名字。

布洛德夫婦旋即報警，沒多久，各家報紙都刊登了麥可的照片和詳細的細節，甚至連全國性的報紙也刊載了這則新聞。然而，沒有任何人認出麥可，或是出面將他領回。於是布洛德夫婦開始照顧麥可，一年後收養了他。

P. 15

麥可跟莎拉和喬治在一起很快樂，而夫婦倆也很開心有麥可陪伴。因為兩人沒有子女，於是麥可彷彿變成他們的親生兒子。

麥可長成一個乖巧的男孩，布洛德店鋪的客人以及麥可在托兒所的朋友師長也很喜歡他。等到麥可年紀漸長懂事之後，莎拉和喬治向他解釋兩人並非他的親生父母，不過，麥可毫不在意。

麥可跟所有小孩一樣，日漸長高變壯，在各方面都很正常，但唯獨胸膛特別大。隨著年齡增長，他的胸膛也變得愈來愈壯碩，進而開始引起別人的注意。老師們開始談論，布洛德夫婦也開始感到納悶。

收養

- 以下這些人物有一個共通性：他們都是被領養長大的小孩。你知道這些人為何赫赫有名嗎？和夥伴討論你們彼此的想法。

  亞里斯多德（Aristotle）
  愛倫坡（Edgar Allan Poe）
  狄更斯（Charles Dickens）
  約翰・藍儂（John Lennon）
  印地安猶長瘋馬（Crazy Horse）
  前南非總統曼德拉（Nelson Mandela）
- 你能想到其他被收養或收養過孩子的名人嗎？

上學

P. 16

在上了小學之後，麥可的生活出現了變化。他肩膀附近的背部開始疼痛，有時夜裡還會痛到無法入睡。家庭醫生替他做了檢查，卻查不出任何異狀。

等到麥可讀小學二年級時，背痛更加劇烈。莎拉於是帶他到醫院看專科醫生。醫生幫他做檢查，拍了 X 光片。醫生從 X 光片上清楚地看到了麥可的肩膀長出了一些多餘的骨頭，就是這些骨頭向外推擠皮膚而導致疼痛的。醫生要莎拉隔天再帶麥可回診，但卻為時已晚。

當天夜裡，莎拉和喬治被麥可臥室裡傳來的尖叫聲所驚醒。他們連忙往麥可的房間奔過去，看到了令他們震驚的一幕——麥可兩邊的肩膀正各自長出一根大骨頭！

喬治打電話叫救護車。一個小時後，麥可回到了醫院。醫院裡的人又幫麥可照了 X 光，有好幾位專科醫生一起會診檢查麥可的身體。喬治和莎拉整晚都待在醫院裡，不時地去探視麥可。在探視的空檔，這群醫生問了他們很多麥可的事。一直到了清晨七點，才有一位護士要他們兩個人先回家。

「那麥可怎麼辦？」喬治問。

「他要住院。」護士回答。

落單的麥可

P. 18

當天上午稍晚，麥可被帶上救護車，轉診到很遠的另一家醫院。

這一天，他哭了。他之所以哭，是因為他的肩膀很痛，是因為他不知道自己身在何處，是因為他的身邊沒有莎拉和喬治陪他。

醫院裡每個人都對麥可很好。他們給他他喜歡吃的食物，唸故事給他聽，還讓他看電視，但他還是很傷。到了晚上，他和莎拉通了電話。

「麥可，別擔心，我們明天就來看你。」莎拉說。

麥可在這家特別的醫院待了一年。他肩膀上的骨頭愈長愈大，周圍也長出了新的肌肉。六個月後，骨頭上開始冒出白色的羽毛，大家都看得出來——包括麥可自己也知道——那是一雙翅膀。慢慢地，他發覺自己可以用胸部的肌肉來移動這些新長出的骨頭。

每天早上都會有一組醫生來幫麥可做檢查，到了下午，則會有其他的醫生來幫助麥可回想被莎拉撿到之前的那段過去。不過，他什麼都想不起來。他不喜歡待在醫院裡，他在這裡唯一喜歡的事，就是上史密斯老師的課，還有，喬治和莎拉每週日都會來探望他。

P. 19

史密斯老師體型瘦小，皮膚黝黑，身穿灰色西裝。他不太教數學或英語，他大部分都在教飛行的事，因為他本身就是一位不折不扣的飛行專家。

他向麥可說明飛行歷史的演變，從達文西如何設計飛行機器做實驗，講解到現代的噴射引擎。麥可認識了鳥類、蝙蝠、昆蟲和飛行動物，學習什麼是風、氣流如何移動，繪製各種模型和圖表，觀看影片，也做實驗。沒多久，麥可也變成了飛行專家。

每天下午，麥可還要去健身室做運動。一位身材高大、名叫彼得的男子會指導他，而史密斯老師和其中一位醫生會從旁觀察做紀錄。麥可所做的運動能夠讓他的胸部和新翅膀的肌肉更結實。一開始，這些運動做起來很辛苦，但慢慢地就不那麼吃力了。

離鄉背井

- 你曾經在沒有家人的陪伴下遠離過家鄉嗎？這是什麼時候的事？你當時有什麼感覺？和夥伴分享一下彼此的經驗。
- 你想，麥可此時會有何等的心情？

麥可開始飛翔

P. 21

在這間特別醫院待了九個月之後，這一天，麥可做了他生平第一次的飛翔。他的翅膀現在已經包覆著長長的美麗白色羽毛。當時他正在健身室做運動，整個人突然騰空了起來，他吃了一驚，嚇得忘記揮動翅膀，結果摔了下來。

「再試一次。」彼得說。於是麥可又試了一次，結果……沒錯！他終於會飛了！

一開始時，他的身體只能抬升到離地面一、兩公尺高，停留在空中的時間只有一分鐘左右，然後就得降落休息。然而，他的肌肉愈來愈強健，一個月之後，他已經能在空中停留好幾分鐘。這真是奇妙的感覺！

從此之後，彼得開始帶麥可到戶外上課，沒多久麥可就學會了如何正確地飛翔。他替史密斯老師感到惋惜，因為老師這麼懂飛行的道理，自己卻飛不起來，而他這樣一個七歲的小男孩卻飛起來了！麥可這時才恍然明白自己與眾不同，跟一般人不一樣：他是一個會飛翔的男孩，而且可能是這個世界上「唯一」會飛翔的男孩。

在接下來的這個星期天，麥可請護士帶喬治和莎拉去醫院大樓旁一座安靜的小花園裡。夫婦倆坐在長椅上等候麥可時，忽然看見麥可往草坪的中央直奔而去。

「嗨，莎拉！嗨，喬治！你們看！」他大聲喊道。

麥可開始揮動他那雙長滿白色羽毛的大翅膀，慢慢地升到半空中。莎拉和喬治不敢相信眼前這一幕，他們看得又哭又笑！

逃離醫院

P. 22

麥可很不想一直待在醫院裡。他想回家，莎拉和喬治也希望他能回家。

「為什麼？我為什麼要待在這裡？我討厭一直住在醫院裡了！我會飛，這又不是什麼毛病！我要回家！」他喊道。

然而，醫生們每天都會找到不同的理由要麥可留在醫院裡。

「他們永遠不可能放我回家，我早晚會變成動物園裡的稀有動物——『一隻會飛的男孩』。」他心想。他一點也不快樂。布洛德夫婦也很不開心，他們不想看到麥可一輩子都住在醫院裡，而是希望他能像同年齡的孩子一樣地生活。於是，莎拉和喬治之後再去探望麥可時，他們三個人想出了一個辦法。

脫逃計畫

- 麥可、喬治和莎拉想出了什麼樣的辦法？找另外兩個夥伴分別扮演這三個角色，討論如何救麥可離開醫院。
- 你們想到的辦法有何利弊？找出可行的方法。

P. 23

在接下來的這個星期天，喬治和莎拉一如往常開車到醫院探視麥可。莎拉下車走進醫院，喬治則把車子開到停車場，坐在車子裡等候。莎拉走到了花園，跟麥可會合。幾分鐘後，她回頭走入醫院，然後對守門人說：「我忘了拿眼鏡，我放在車上了。」

守門人打開大門讓莎拉出去。莎拉走到停車場，鑽入車子裡。一會兒後，麥可飛越醫院的高牆，降落在停車場，收起翅膀，也鑽入車內。喬治隨即猛踩油門，快速駛離醫院，揚長而去。

家有難題

P. 24

醫院的守門人打電話報警，警局裡有人通知了報社。喬治才一回到家，車子馬上被國內各家報社、電視台、電台的攝影師和記者團團圍住。他們三個人根本無法避開記者和狗仔隊的騷擾而順利下車。人群此起彼落地喊道：

「布洛德太太，能否請妳對這男孩的精神狀態說幾句話？」

「布洛德先生，你認為這男孩的親生母親是誰？」

「嘿！麥可！飛行的感覺怎樣？」

「麥可，你現在最想做的事是什麼？」

麥可、莎拉、喬治從人群中奮力擠出一條路才進到了屋裡。他們很惶恐，家裡的電話一直響個不停，人群不斷敲打大門，有些攝影師甚至闖入後花園，開始對屋裡拍照。莎拉拉下窗簾，他們站在屋裡，面面相覷。這次回家，對麥可來說一點也不溫馨。

「喬治，我們該怎麼辦？」莎拉問丈夫。

「我也不知道。」喬治回答。

這時，大門突然傳來一聲很大的敲門聲，接著有一個聲音喊道：

「布洛德先生，請開門，我們是警察！」

P. 26

喬治打開大門，看見兩位高大的員警、一位便衣督察和一位從醫院來的醫生，其他警察則正把所有的媒體人推回街道上。

喬治讓督察和醫生進入屋內，兩位穿制服的員警則守在門外。

「你們這麼做很不對，我們告訴過你們，麥可不能回家。」醫生說。

「可是他在醫院裡已經待不下去了，他需要回家和我們住在一起，過正常生活——去上學、和朋友玩……」莎拉說。

「布洛德太太，這我知道。可是麥可不是一般的小孩，你也看到外面的情況了，他需要保護，才不會被外界給騷擾。」醫生回答。

「我不要在醫院裡過一輩子！我又沒有病，我想過跟別的孩子一樣的生活。」麥可喊道。

麥可的未來

- 你覺得麥可的父母、醫生和警方督察替麥可做了什麼樣的決定？
- 想像你是以下這些人，你覺得怎麼做對麥可才是最好的？
  莎拉・布洛德　　喬治・布洛德
  麥可的醫生　　警方

P. 27

「這個我知道，麥可。可是我們必須保護你，這樣那些記者或是任何想利用或傷害你的人，才不會得逞。」醫生說。

「傷害他？他不過是個小孩子。」喬治問。

「是沒錯，但他是世界上唯一有翅膀的小孩子！我們要確保他不會遇到不好的事情。」醫生回答。

「你們只想把他留在醫院裡做研究，根本不在乎他是個人。」莎拉說。

「布洛德太太，有一點你說得沒錯。麥可不是一般人，世界各地的科學家對他的發展都很感興趣。不過，我可以向你保證，我們把他當成人，很關心他的情況。」醫生說。

布洛德夫婦跟醫生與警方督察談了一整個晚上。麥可先進臥室睡覺，此時，樓下的人們正決定著他的未來。

改變

P. 28

隔天一早，布洛德先生繞路到當地的報攤買早報。

「早安，約翰。」他向報攤的人打招呼。

「早，喬治。出名的感覺怎麼樣啊？」對方笑著問道。

「什麼意思？」喬治驚訝地問。

「你看看所有這些報紙的頭版！而且我昨晚還在電視上看到你。」報攤老闆回答。

喬治望著報架上的全國性報紙，舉目

所見都是自己、太太和麥可的照片，而且大大的標題寫著「麥可飛回家」和「超級男孩終於返家！」

「麥可現在是大明星了。喬治，你就要發了！」報攤老闆說。

「約翰，別說了！拜託今天的報紙全部都給我一份。」喬治生氣地說。

喬治一回到家，第一批記者早已在守在房子外頭，他們丟出一連串的問題問喬治：

「布洛德先生，你今天替麥可安排了什麼計畫？」

「我們什麼時候可以看麥可飛？」

「兒子這麼與眾不同，你有何感想？」

喬治不予理會。

P. 30

「你看這個！」他把報紙放在餐桌上對莎拉說：「到處都是我們的照片跟報導。」

「噢！不會吧！」她鬱悶地說。

吃早餐時，夫婦倆向麥可說明他們如何規劃他的未來。

早上稍晚時，兩位醫生抵達麥可家。他們帶麥可穿過那些還在大聲發問、猛按快門的記者群，送他上救護車，然後把他送回醫院。

麥可在醫院裡待了一個月。後來，一個星期一的上午，麥可期盼的警車終於來醫院接他。一位警員把麥可的行李放入後車廂，接著進入後座，坐在他身旁。他們開了一整天的車，沿途只停過一次買東西吃。到了下午五點左右，麥可看到一塊寫著「蘇格蘭」的路標，又過了一、兩個鐘頭之後，他看到了大海。警車停在海岸上一個偏僻的地方，那裡有一艘船在等候他們，麥可隨後跟警察上了船。這是他生平第一次搭船，他感到興奮不已。

麥可正前往一座島嶼，那裡離海岸約一小時的船程。這座島嶼叫作「喜兒蘭」，喬治和莎拉早已在島上等候他。他們三個人開心地走向一棟房子，那裡即將成為他們的新家。進了屋子之後，布洛德夫婦帶著麥可看了看各個房間。麥可的臥室很大，可以看到美麗的海景，而且他的玩具和書本都已經擺放在裡頭。

這麼多個月以來，這是他第一次打從心裡感到快樂。

喜兒蘭島上的新生活

P. 31

隔天早上七點半，麥可的新生活正式展開。他起床後，在又大又溫暖的廚房裡跟喬治與莎拉一同吃早餐。到了九點，一位名叫理查・李德的醫生來到家裡，帶麥可到一間擺設著各種特殊設備的實驗室。李德醫生替麥可拍照、量體重、量身體尺寸，並且把所有資料輸入電腦。

九點半時，麥可被帶到一間房間，裡面擺著書籍、紙張、顏料、工具、科學設備、電腦、電視、影音光碟機，還有一張舒適的大書桌。

「這是你的教室。」醫生說。

麥可坐在書桌前，李德醫生教他如何打開電腦。

「現在把耳機戴上，按第十台。」醫生說。

麥可按了一下第十台的圖示，螢幕上出現了兩個坐在桌前的人。

「早安！麥可。」他們兩個人同時向麥可打招呼。

P. 32

「我叫莎莉・羅伯茲。」其中一位女士笑著說：「他叫保羅・布朗，我們是你的老師，你可以用耳機上的麥克風跟我們通話。」

每一天，這兩位老師都會單獨或共同指導麥可，教他學習數學、英語、歷史等等學校會教的學科。麥可會用電子郵件把作業寄給莎莉或保羅，然後他們會和麥可討論作業，並幫他解惑。

學校

- 你在學校讀的是什麼？
- 所有的科目都是必修的嗎？還是你可以自己選修？
- 你想嘗試麥可的學習方式嗎？

十一點十五分時，他會去廚房找喬治和莎拉，跟他們一起喝個東西，吃吃餅乾，然後再繼續做更多的功課，一直到下午一點才結束。在用過午餐後，如果天氣好，他會出門散步。

麥可通常喜歡自己一個人去散步，不過有時喬治和莎拉會陪他。他每個星期要做兩份喜兒蘭島上的生物研究報告，隔天要交給老師。

P. 33

接近傍晚時，李德醫生會回到布洛德的家，和麥可來到小型健身室。每天下午四點到四點半，麥可都要做運動，李德醫生會在一旁攝影。麥可所要做的運動，包括一般學童在學校會做的運動，還有李德醫生特別要求的運動，以鍛鍊他的翅膀和胸肌。

到了晚上，麥可會打電腦遊戲、看電視、跟莎拉與喬治玩紙牌等各種遊戲，或是讀教室圖書室裡的書。

喜兒蘭是一座小島，南端有一個小港口，供抵達的船隻停靠，李德醫生住的小屋就位在那裡。麥可的家則位在小島的東邊，房子後方有一片叫做「島主森林」的松樹林，和一座叫做「鵝湖」的湖泊。冬天時，野雁野鵝會來湖中戲水、覓食。喜兒蘭島南部的地勢很平坦，盡是草原，但北部就丘陵遍布。島嶼的西北方有兩座山，一座叫「城堡山」，因為山頂矗立著一座城堡廢墟；另一座叫「峭壁山」，因為那座山特別多岩石。島嶼上野花遍布，而且有一些稀有的花卉品種。

P. 34

沒多久，麥可對這座島嶼的每吋土地已瞭如指掌，島上大部分的花朵、鳥類和動物，他都已經能辨識。剛開始的時候，他還很懷念以前的玩伴，但時間久了，他也習慣了獨自一人玩耍。

莎拉和喬治很滿意這裡的新生活。他們不用再經營店鋪，有時間從事自己喜歡的活動。喬治開墾了一個菜園，莎拉則投入野花的繪畫。莎拉在繪畫和做家事之餘，也會幫麥可縫製衣服。她替麥可設計了一件特大號的夾克，夾克好穿又好脱，而且可以蓋住他的翅膀。

P. 35

麥可有時候會飛翔。他從家裡飛到島嶼的北端，只需要十五分鐘。他飛行的技巧日漸純熟，可以愈飛愈高、愈飛愈久。這一個星期六，是他滿八歲的日子，他在午餐時間回到家時説：「喬治，你知道嗎，我今天早上繞著小島的海岸飛了一圈！我中途停了四次，不過都只休息一下下而已。」

喬治和莎拉聽了很吃驚，不過後來一想，他們知道，飛行對麥可來説，不過就像其他的孩子騎長途單車或踢足球一樣。

P. 36

布洛德夫婦和麥可就這樣幸福地度過一天又一天。每個月都會有一艘船載運食物等必需品來給他們，除此之外，島上就見不到其他人了。他們看著四季更迭交替。冬天時，惡劣的海象有時很駭人，而且通常會降下幾場大雪；夏天時，氣候晴朗，白晝很長，晚上十點時日照還很亮。

逐漸地，麥可愈長愈高、愈長愈壯。他上課時很認真，現在是一個聰明伶俐的男孩。喬治和莎拉很欣慰他們當初決定搬到喜兒蘭，因為麥可可以逃離社會大眾的目光，健康地成長。

你的家

- 你住在哪裡？勾選以下的選項：
  - ☐ 住在大城市
  - ☐ 住在城填上
  - ☐ 住在小鄉鎮
  - ☐ 住在鄉下
- 與夥伴討論你居住的地方有什麼優點和缺點。

計畫

P. 38

麥克轉眼已經十二歲了，這一天晚上，李德醫師來訪，想跟他們討論一些事情。

「我在倫敦的老闆打了一通電話給我，他說，英國廣播公司問說可不可以幫麥克拍個紀錄片。」他說。

莎拉露出愁容，因為她對記者、攝影師和電視人員的印象還很不好。

「我覺得這個想法不太妥當。」莎拉說。

「莎拉，先別急，我們先聽聽醫師的說法。理查，你說吧。」

「《奇情人間》這個節目的製片人，想在新的帶狀節目中為麥可拍一部四十五分鐘的紀錄片。」理查解釋道：「我的老闆覺得這個想法還不錯，麥可要長大成人了，不能一輩子都只待在這個小島上。我們應該讓麥克認識一下英國的人們，這樣他以後才可以選個什麼地方過一般人的生活——像是上大學、找工作等等的。」

「我同意你的說法，但是現在就這樣做會不會有點危險？麥可還很小啊！」喬治說道。

「我想拍！電視上的《奇情人間》我們每一集都有看，這個節目很好。」麥可說。

電視

- 你喜歡看電視嗎？
- 你最喜歡看的節目是什麼？
- 你自己會想上電視嗎？
- 你覺得麥可的決定妥當嗎？

P. 39

「沒錯！這個節目的製作群是一群很認真的人，節目在播出之前，我們一定會先審查過影片，確保內容沒有問題。」醫生同意地說道。

「不過他們不能在這個島上拍影片，這太冒險了！」莎拉說：「我怕這個地方被認出來，然後那些報紙記者就會跑過來。」

「那是當然的，他們一定要另外找個地方來拍。」李德醫生說。

「可是我還是覺得這樣做不妥當。」莎拉看著喬治說道。

「理查，你覺得呢？這樣做，對麥可會不會太冒險了？」喬治問。

「我覺得不會。」理查回答：「另外還有一點，這是一個重點，如果麥可願意拍紀錄片，英國廣播公司會給麥可一萬塊錢的英鎊當作片酬。」

「哇！那我不就可以……可以買任何東西了！」麥可說。

「是的，沒錯！」醫師笑笑地說道：「能幫麥可在銀行裡存些錢，讓他以後可以用，這個想法也不錯。」

「你這樣說也是對的。」莎拉說。

「那我要請我的老闆開始做安排了嗎？」李德醫生問。

布洛德夫婦看看麥可，然後彼此又對視了一下，都點點了頭。

「那好，我明天就會和老闆談。」醫生說：「現在，我們何不來玩玩撲克牌？」

拍片

P. 41

五月的這一天早上，一架警方的直昇機飛來島上載他們。莎拉、喬治、麥可和李德醫生在草原上等待直昇機降落。他們爬上機內，直昇機隨即起飛。這天的天氣很晴朗，山脈、湖泊、河谷的景色非常美麗。到了正午，直昇機降落在一座荒廢的機場上。

「這裡以前是一個重要的軍事中心，但現在已經停用了。」一行人走向一些建築物時，李德醫生向大家做了說明：「我的老闆會挑上這裡，是因為這裡離喜兒蘭很遠，而且沒有人煙。還有，多年前用來停放飛機的大機棚，剛好可以用來拍攝麥可的飛行。」

英國廣播公司的人員已經在機棚等候。李德醫生逐一介紹眾人後，《奇情人間》節目的製作人保羅・沙特邀請他們共用午餐。

「我們想拍一些跟你們大家的訪談，我們這邊只有四個人。瑪莉將負責訪問你們，史帝夫是攝影師，傑夫負責音效和燈光，再加上我。我們希望大家都能盡量放鬆，所以全程的訪談都會在這個房間裡進行。等晚一點，我們再移到機棚，拍攝麥可的飛行。」保羅說。

P. 42

午餐過後，英國廣播公司團隊架好設備。就在第一次訪談開始前，李德醫生轉向喬治、莎拉和麥可，說道：「記住，千萬別提到喜兒蘭！連我們住在島上或住在蘇格蘭，也不要說！不要讓英國廣播公司的人知道我們住在哪裡，可以嗎？」

他們三個人點了點頭。

在接下來的兩天，喬治、莎拉、麥可和李德醫生四人分別以單獨、兩人和全體的方式接受訪問。到了第三天的午餐時間，保羅・沙特召集大家聚在一起。

「非常感謝各位的配合，我們已經拍了很精彩的訪談內容。今天下午就請大家好好休息，明天早上我們再進機棚拍攝麥可飛行的英姿。」他說。

訪談

- 跟一個夥伴合作，列出你們想問麥可的問題，和全班分享，並選出五個最好的問題。
- 跟夥伴輪流扮演麥可和訪問者的角色，並問完所有問題。
- 在課堂上將訪談過程表演出來。

P. 43

當天下午，趁著布洛德夫婦在休息、李德醫生與保羅・沙特在交談時，麥可外出散步。他走近直昇機想看個清楚，這時聽到身後傳來了腳步聲——是傑夫。

「嘿，小麥！你在幹嘛呀？」他說。

「看看直昇機而已。」麥可冷淡地回答。他不喜歡別人叫他小麥。

「你看過舊式的飛機嗎？」傑夫對他示好。

「什麼飛機？」

「這裡有一些舊式的戰鬥機，想不想看啊？」傑夫說。

「好啊，在哪裡？」麥可說。

「在二號機棚。小麥，你喜歡接受那些訪談嗎？」傑夫回答。

「一開始還好，後來就覺得有點無聊。」麥可說。

「那我想你一定很期待明天了。」這位燈光音效技術員說。

「為什麼？」麥可一臉困惑地問。

「因為明天你就要飛行了啊，不是嗎？那一定很刺激。」

「對別人來說，或許是吧。」麥可說。

「你會飛，學校的同學有說什麼嗎？」傑夫用奇怪的眼神盯著麥可的臉問道。

P. 44

「他們沒說什麼。」麥可回答。

「怎麼會？」

「那裡沒有學校，在喜兒……上」麥可差點說溜嘴，連忙閉嘴。

「喜兒？那在哪裡？我沒聽過喜兒這個地方。」傑夫問。

「呃……它在……呃……它……」麥可支支吾吾，滿臉脹紅。「我要回去了，傑夫，很晚了。」

麥可轉身跑開，技術員在他背後望著他離去。「在喜兒……上，在喜兒……上。」他喃喃自語著。

英國廣播公司人員在機棚拍攝麥可的飛行，工作進行得很順利，結束時剛好是午餐時間。當天晚上七點，布洛德夫婦、麥可和李德醫生回到了喜兒蘭島。

傑夫的朋友

P. 45

瘦皮猴威爾森書房裡的電話響起，他關掉電視，接起電話。

「瘦皮猴嗎？」

「什麼事？」

「我是傑夫，傑夫・杭特。」

「哈囉，傑夫。有消息嗎？」

「有，我想我找到了一條線索，我過去找你好嗎？」

「好，七點半來，彼得斯也會到。」

傑夫按了門鈴，威爾森開門讓他進來。彼得斯這位體型壯碩的禿頭男子，也已經坐在沙發上。

「有什麼消息？」威爾森問。

「瘦皮猴，那個男孩真是行啊，我們的工作就需要這種人。他這一秒站在地面上，結果他翅膀一揮，下一秒就咻地飛起來了！真是難以置信！」傑夫說。

「你查出他住在哪裡了嗎？」彼得斯問。

「要套他們的話很難，他們口風很緊。

不過我有一天找男孩單獨講了話，他有提到一個地名，但沒講完整。」傑夫回答。

「他說什麼？」威爾森問。

「他說『那裡沒有學校，在喜兒……上』。」

「喜兒在哪裡？」威爾森追問。

「我也不知道。我有問他，但他不肯說。我回家拿了地圖查，也沒找著。」傑夫說。

P. 46

威爾森走到書架前，抽出一本大型的世界地圖集，裡頭有詳盡的英國地圖。他瀏覽了索引。

「英國沒有叫喜兒的地方，搞不好是別的國家的地名。」他說。

「有可能，不過我覺得喜兒不是完整的地名。」傑夫說。

威爾森又檢視了索引，將地名逐一唸出來：「喜兒伯特、喜兒登、喜兒蘭、喜兒佛德有三個、喜兒林斯敦……，有很多地名的開頭都是喜兒。」

「我們來看看這些地點在地圖上的哪裡，他不可能住在城鎮或大城市，一定是一個小地方。」傑夫說。

他們三個人在地圖上查看所有地點的位置，討論最有可能的地點。

「喜兒摩爾住在英格蘭北部的山丘上，那裡一定很小，因為我家裡的地圖上沒有。」傑夫說。

「沒錯，那裡只有兩、三間房子，你看。」彼得斯指著地圖說。

「喜兒騰尼西看起來更小，它位在蘇格蘭，離其他地方都很遠。還有，有一個叫喜兒蘭的地方，是靠近蘇格蘭西海岸的一座島嶼。」傑夫說。

「你覺得呢？瘦皮猴。」彼得斯問。

「傑夫，你再說一次，那個男孩說了什麼？」威爾森說。

「他說『那裡沒有學校，在喜兒……上』」傑夫回答。

麥可的藏身處

- 威爾森如何得知麥可住在喜兒蘭島上？
- 傑夫提供的哪條線索給了威爾森答案？

P. 47

「啊，答案出現了！」威爾森笑道。

傑夫和彼得斯兩人一臉困惑。

「怎麼說？」彼得斯問。

「那個男孩說，『那裡沒有學校，在喜兒……上』！」威爾森解釋說：「『在喜兒……上』，他還是說溜嘴，多說了一個『上』。提到山岳島嶼時，才會說『上』。喜兒摩爾是山上的一個村莊，它本身不是山；喜兒騰尼西在一座島上，它本身不是島。而喜兒蘭是一座島！『在喜兒蘭上沒有學校』——這是麥可原本想說的話！」

其他兩人望著威爾森。

「恭喜你啊，福爾摩斯！」彼得斯一說完，大家都笑了。

在島上

- 麥可住在一座島「上」。請在以下空格填入正確的介系詞，完成句子。

喜兒蘭上的訪客

P. 48

拍完紀錄片返家後，他們在喜兒蘭上的生活又回歸正常。過了幾個星期，英國廣播公司寄來了紀錄片的一份拷貝帶。當天傍晚，李德醫生與布洛德夫婦坐著觀看影片。看到自己出現在影片上，這種感覺讓他們感到怪怪的。

「大家都做得很好！我們順利完成訪問，都沒提到我們住的地方。我明天就向老闆報告，說我們同意英國廣播公司在電視上播放這支影片。」李德醫生說。

當天夜裡，三個男人搭乘小橡皮艇，從喜兒蘭的東海灘登陸。他們把船藏在岩塊後面，並用沙灘上撿來的木頭遮蓋住。

P. 50

他們點燃火把查看地圖。

「沒錯，我們要往北走。」威爾森說。

傑夫・杭特看了看手中的羅盤說：「往這邊走。」

他們沿著小路走，一直走到峭壁山，接著轉西前往城堡山。

「到了，就是這裡！」威爾森說。

他們悄悄沿著山邊往上走，當他們抵達山頂的城堡廢墟時，天色才正要破曉。

彼得斯隔著城牆往下看，說道：「這個地點很好，往山下看去，一覽無遺。」

P. 51

三名男子

- 想想看，這三名男子是誰？
- 他們打算做什麼？與夥伴分享你的看法。

早上的課程結束後，麥可下樓走進廚房吃午餐，這時莎拉正從烤箱拿出一盤烤魚派。

「這魚是李德醫生昨天抓的，麻煩你去叫喬治來吃！」她說。

吃完午餐，麥可站起來，給莎拉一個緊緊的擁抱，說道：「真好吃！我向主廚致上萬分的敬意！」

莎拉笑了。

「我現在出門去做生物學的作業，待會見！」他提起帆布背包，走出門，沐浴在溫暖的陽光之中。

他選擇通往鵝湖的路徑，他現在正在做鵝湖四周濕草區的植物研究報告。那裡有一些稀有品種，他把它們生長的位置畫成一張圖。

「他在那裡！」傑夫對威爾森說。

P. 53

「他正沿著湖邊的路走，你們看！」

威爾森拿起雙筒望遠鏡，湊近眼睛觀看，他看到麥可正走到鵝湖的北端。

「他停下來了，他掏出一本書在寫東西。」威爾森說。

「你看他是在幹嘛？」彼得斯問。

「我也不知道，我猜他在草堆中看到了什麼，正在做筆記。」威爾森回答。

他們看了好一陣子，麥可繼續做著筆記。

傑夫突然說：「好啦，你們準備好了嗎？」

「準備好了。彼得斯，你們拿槍了嗎？」威爾森說。

「拿了，在這裡！」彼得斯答道。

「現在，把東西帶上，我們走！」

他們三個人躡手躡腳，偷偷地從城堡山的側邊下山，然後朝麥可的方向穿越草地。他們來到離他兩百公尺時，停下腳步，俯臥趴在地上。彼得斯把槍架好，然後三人靜靜地等待著。

P.55

過了一會，麥可把書本收進背包站起來。彼得斯瞄準後開槍。麥可痛得大叫一聲，隨即倒地。他們三個人站起來，跑向昏倒在地的男孩。彼得斯從麥可的左手臂拔出一根小飛鏢，然後幫傑夫把他抬起。他們抬著麥可，繞著鵝湖，走進島主森林。

他們要找個藏身之處，等到天黑，而樹林是最理想的地點。他們一直走，最後來到林中深處一塊長滿草的小空地。

他們把昏迷不醒的麥可放在地上，然後在旁邊坐下。

「瘦皮猴，你覺得我們什麼時候離開才安全？」傑夫問。

「我想至少要等到晚上九點，北方夏季的天色很晚才會變黑。」威爾森說。

「所以我們得在這裡待六小時左右。」傑夫說。

「沒錯。晚上十點時，船會回來接應我們。彼得斯，安眠藥的藥效能持續多久？」威爾森回答。

「十二個小時。」彼得斯回答。

「很好！我們就坐在這裡等，希望他們還不會開始尋找麥可。」威爾森說。

P.56

接下來會發生什麼事？

- 你想，接下來會發生什麼事？選擇下面的情況：
  - a. 麥可會在他們離開小島之前醒來，然後逃離那三個人的掌心。
  - b. 三個人綁架麥可是為了向喬治和莎拉勒索。
  - c. 三個人要麥可為他們幹偷竊勾當。
  - d. 三個人要麥可教他們如何飛行。
  - e. 三個人當中有一個是麥可的生父，他想要認兒子。
- 鋪陳接下來的劇情。

麥可失蹤了

P. 57

下午三點五十分時，莎拉開始準備下午茶。她泡了一壺茶，並在餐桌上放了一些蛋糕。麥可下午散步回到家時，會又餓又渴。四點整，李德醫生也會來一起享用下午茶。

「莎拉，今天天氣真好。」莎拉讓醫生進入廚房時，醫生說道：「這是今年夏天數一數二的好天氣。」

「是啊。理查，請坐，麥可很快就回來了。我去叫喬治，他還在菜園裡工作。」莎拉說。

「莎拉，老實說，他在花園的椅子上曬太陽，睡得正熟呢。」醫生說。

莎拉倒茶時，兩人都笑了。

兩人一邊等待，一邊喝、吃蛋糕，聊著天。到了四點半，莎拉站起身，來到窗邊。

「麥可平時不會這麼晚回來的。」她說。

「莎拉，先別擔心。他去哪裡了？」李德醫生說。

「我不清楚，他有一些作業要做。」她回答。

兩人又等了十五分鐘，這時喬治走了進來。

「哈囉，理查。親愛的莎拉，還有沒有剩啊？」喬治說。

「喬治，麥可還沒回來。」莎拉說。

P. 58

「還沒回來嗎？我想他一定還在賞鳥。」丈夫答道。

「我去查他的電腦，看看他今天的作業是什麼。」李德醫生說完便走上樓，幾分鐘後又回到廚房。

「他在研究鵝湖北邊的植物，我去看看他在那裡做什麼。」他說。

理查・李德花了二十分鐘才走到鵝湖。他四處尋找，喊了幾聲「麥可」，但都沒有回應。醫生感到很疑惑，因為這不像麥可的作風，麥可用餐是不會遲到的。下午茶一向都在四點，而現在已經五點半了。

「你有聽到嗎？」傑夫說。

「什麼？」威爾森坐直身子問。

「你聽！」傑夫回說。

他們聽到一個男人在大喊麥可。

「是醫生，李德醫生。」傑夫說。

他們安靜坐著聽動靜，醫生又喊了兩聲。

李德醫生返回莎拉的房子，期盼看到麥可已經回到家，但是廚房裡只有莎拉和喬治。莎拉開始哭了起來。

P. 59

「親愛的，別擔心，他很快就會回來了。」喬治伸出一隻手，環抱著她說：「他可能是看到了什麼有趣的事，所以擔擱了時間。」

喬治的心裡其實也很擔心，因為麥可一向很可靠的。

「我現在去城堡山山頂看看，從山頂上我就能看到他。喬治，我可以向你借雙筒望遠鏡嗎？」李德醫生說。

「當然！，你等等，我跟你一起去！。」他回答。

他們兩人出發，沿著小徑快步行走，

現在已經晚上七點，但日光仍然閃耀，氣候溫暖。他們不時各自喊著麥可的名字，除此之外，兩個人行走時都默不作聲。

被囚禁

P. 60

麥可醒來後，發現自己處在一個又小又暗的地方。他被塞進一個箱子裡，雙手被綑綁在背後。他知道自己一定在汽車或廂型車裡，因為車子轉彎時，他人被甩向了另一邊。他感到很迷惑，不過後來就開始明白了起來。

「我記得我當時在研究花朵，然後手臂突然感到疼痛，接著眼前就一片漆黑了。我現在在哪裡？我是怎麼進到這裡的？我會被載去哪裡？」

經過好長一段時間後，這輛汽車或廂型車終於停下來。麥可聽到了聲音。

「救命！」他使盡全力地大叫：「救命啊！」

P. 61

瘦皮猴威爾森緊張地看著傑夫和彼得斯。

「他醒了，我們快把他抬進來。」威爾森說。

彼得斯打開廂型車的後門，三人合力抬出一個大箱子。在廂型車裡還有好幾個類似的箱子。

「放我出去！」麥可大聲吼道，不過三人並不理會。

他們把箱子抬進一棟建築物裡的一個小房間裡，然後把箱子放在地上。

「麥可，你仔細聽好。」威爾森把臉貼近箱子，說道：「我們要你去執行一項任務，如果你順利完成了，我們就放你走。要是你失敗了，我們就殺了莎拉·布洛德。她也在這裡，就在另一個房間裡。這樣你懂嗎？」

「我懂！可是先放我出去，我很渴！」麥可說道。

威爾森向彼得斯和杭特比了個動作，兩人隨即打開箱子，把麥可從裡面拉出來，放到椅子上。當麥可看到這些人時，他嚇壞了：他們都戴著全罩式頭套，其中一個人手裡握著一瓶水。

「請幫我把手鬆開。」麥可說。

「那你得答應聽話，別忘了，我說過莎拉會有什麼樣的下場。」威爾森說。

「我會聽話。」麥可說。

P. 62

威爾森點了點頭，彼得斯割斷繩索，麥可拿了水喝。而就在威爾森還來不及反應之前，麥可把水瓶砸向他，然後跳起來，張開翅膀，咻地飛上了天花板。

「把他抓下來！」威爾森大喊道。

他們三個人奮力想抓住在房間繞著飛行的麥可。最後，彼得斯爬上桌子，抓住麥可的腿，把他扯了下來。

「你要是敢再逃，莎拉就死定了！把他的翅膀綁起來，看他怎麼飛！」威爾森氣呼呼地吼道。

彼得斯和杭特拿來了繩索，把麥可的翅膀和身體緊緊纏住。

「現在你給我聽好！剛剛的話我再講一遍，我們要你替我們做一件簡單的工作，做完就放你走。我們不想傷害你，也不想傷害你媽媽，懂嗎？如果你乖乖聽我們的話，一切都會沒事。所以你要不要當個乖孩子？」威爾森說。

麥可點了點頭。

麥可

- 你想麥可此時的心情是怎樣的？閉上眼睛，想像你自己是麥可，然後說明你的感覺，回答下面的問題：
  1. 你在哪裡？
  2. 你會害怕嗎？
  3. 你的身體感到痛楚嗎？
  4. 那些人是什麼人？
  5. 他們會要你做什麼事？

P. 64

威爾森看著傑夫說：「現在先給他吃點東西，我們待會再告訴他要做什麼。」

傑夫拿了一些三明治給麥可。傑夫沒有開口，但麥可很確定他認識這個人，因為他的動作看起來有點熟悉。過了一會，他帶著麥可走去另一個房間，裡頭放著一台電腦。

「麥可，坐下，好好看這支影片。」威爾森說。

麥可看著影片。影片裡頭有一面很高的牆，每隔幾百公尺就有一個警衛站哨。接著是鳥瞰高牆的鏡頭，牆內是一大群建築物。鏡頭開始向建築物拉近，看起來好像是辦公室。

「聽好，麥可，在那棟大樓裡有一個我很想要的東西，所以我才需要你的幫忙。我要你飛過那面牆，替我到裡面拿個東西。現在你過來這裡看看這些平面圖。」威爾森說。

他帶麥可走到角落的一張大桌子旁，桌上擺了大樓的平面圖。

「你從這棟建築物進去。」威爾森指著第一張平面圖上的一個紅色正方形，說道：「房子的內部看起來就像這樣子。」他秀了一個房間的平面圖給麥可看。「你走進這個房間，打開這個櫃子，然後拿出正面寫著『獅子』兩個字的信封。」

接下來的兩個鐘頭，威爾森一步一步詳細地指導麥可該如何行動。

搜尋開始

P. 65

在喜兒蘭島上，布洛德夫婦和李德醫生打電話向警方報案。警方搭乘直昇機抵達，開始對島嶼展開搜索。隔天早上，搜救隊在東海灘的沙中發現腳印以及橡皮艇留下的痕跡。

接近正午時，萊理警探來到布洛德夫婦家中，向他們說明最新的情況。

「現在我們確定麥可不在這個島上，而且他是被人用橡皮艇帶走的。」他說。

「我求求你們趕快把他找回來！」莎拉啜泣地說。

「我們會的。布洛德太太，別擔心！」萊理語氣溫和地說，「我們已經派菁英員警在調查了。」

「是誰綁走了麥可，你們有任何頭緒嗎？」喬治問。

「是有一些，你們唯一接觸過的人，就是英國廣播公司的那四個人。我們已經跟其中三個談過了，但是目前為止還找不到杭特。」萊理回答。

「你是說傑夫？」李德醫生問。

「沒錯，就是那個技術員。」萊理回答。

「那現在我們能做什麼？」喬治問。

「現在還無法有任何動作，但我們已經把這個案件列為最優先處理，希望你們不要太擔心。」萊理回答。

闖入

P. 66

翌日清晨，彼得斯把麥可的美麗白色羽毛染黑。

「這樣你在夜裡飛行就不容易被看見。」

在等待染料乾的同時，威爾森在麥可的腰部綁上一條腰帶，在上面裝了兩個電子儀器：一個是讓麥可用來和威爾森交談的發送器，另一個則是爆炸裝置。

「麥可，你要是敢搞鬼，這個裝置就會爆炸，那你就會死掉，莎拉・布洛德也會死掉！」威爾森說道，接著交給麥可一個麥克風和耳機，搭配發送器使用。威爾森要他跟隔壁房裡的彼得斯先練習通訊，以便檢查通話系統是否正常。

下午三點左右，麥可穿上了黑色夾克、黑色長褲和黑色頭套。現在他可以確定其中一個人就是在英國廣播公司工作的傑夫，即使傑夫未開口說話，其他人也從未提起這個名字。

下午五點，這夥人帶著麥可出發前往「政府核子研究中心」。他們逼麥可鑽回箱子，再把箱子搬上廂型車。他的翅膀仍然被緊緊綁住，這讓他很難受。他們開了大約四個小時，最後廂型車終於停下，麥可被放出來，讓他一時覺得很高興。

P. 67

「研究中心就在那裡。」威爾森指著上方架有一些探照燈的高牆說：「麥可！接著你知道要做什麼，還有不遵照指示的後果，對不對？」

「我知道。」麥可回答。他很害怕，但沒有顯露出來。他不想幫助這些歹徒從政府大樓竊取機密文件，而且也不想被警衛發現射殺。

「很好。好啦，你們兩個，把他的翅膀鬆開！」威爾森說。

傑夫和彼得斯解開繩子，麥可的翅膀張開閉合了幾次。威爾森看了一下手錶。

「好，九點四十五分，麥可，在你趁警衛換班時溜進去還有十五分鐘，我們現

在來檢查電子設備。」他說。

傑夫走過來，打開麥可腰帶上的各項儀器，接著檢查威爾森和彼得斯的監控螢幕，所有人全都測試了麥克風和耳機的運作是否正常。

「謝謝你，傑夫。」麥可趁彼得斯與威爾森在幾公尺外交談時輕聲地說。

「沒什麼。呃，你剛說什麼？」傑夫問，臉上露出驚訝的表情。

「我說：『謝謝你，傑夫。』」麥可回答。

P. 69

「你怎麼知道……呃，我不叫傑夫。我叫……呃……史帝夫。」杭特回答，但語氣沒什麼說服力。

「失禮了，史帝夫，你讓我想起我認識的一個人。」麥可說。

「準備好了嗎？」威爾森一邊走向麥可和杭特，一邊問道。

「好了，一切運作正常。」傑夫回答。

「很好，麥可，該你行動了。」威爾森說。

麥可起飛後，往高空直沖而上，在三個人的上方繞著大圈子飛行。他愈飛愈高，愈飛愈高，很快就飛到了探照燈光束的上方。他在空中盤旋時，想過降落在庭院裡，把真相告訴警衛，說「有一幫歹徒挾持我，要我從這裡偷走重要的東西。拜託你救救我！」

但是不行，他不能這麼做。這群歹徒透過發送器監視著他的一舉一動。他該怎麼辦？他想了又想，還是沒想出辦法，他決定進到大樓內部之後，再靜觀其變。

警方逼近

P. 70

「有消息嗎？」萊理結束一通很長的電話、走回到客廳時，喬治問他。時間是下午四點。幾百公里之外，那幫歹徒正準備出發前往核子研究中心。

「有。我們搜索了傑夫的公寓，查看了他的電子郵件。他在信裡提到英格蘭北方的一個『目標』，還說它『很遠』。我們認為這些人之所以挾持麥可，是要他飛入一個被高牆或類似結構包圍的地方。我們過濾出在英格蘭北部的這種地點有四處，現在我們正派警員趕往每一個地點。我們還找到了跟傑夫用電子郵件來往的人的住所。」警探說。

「沒有麥可的任何消息嗎？」莎拉問。

「目前還沒有，不過就快要水落石出了。」萊理回答。

就在此時，萊理的行動電話響了。「抱歉。」他說完後走出屋外，五分鐘後回到屋裡，臉上帶著奇怪的表情。

「好消息嗎？還是壞消息？」喬治問。

「都有。杭特電子郵件的聯絡人叫艾德華・威爾森，綽號『瘦皮猴』。這是好消息，因為我們現在知道要追查誰了。」萊理回答。

「那壞消息呢？」喬治問。

P. 71

「威爾森是一個出名的國際罪犯，我們查看了他的電腦，發現他正在跟一個重要的恐怖組織合作。英格蘭北方的『目標』，就是恐怖分子要的東西，他們願意拿大筆金錢來換取。」

「天啊，麥可被捲進去了！」喬治說。

「是沒錯，不過這讓我們更容易推斷可能犯案的地點。我們認為他們想闖入約克附近的瓦菲德軍事武器機構，或是里茲市外的政府核子研究中心。所以我們已經調派大部分人力前往這兩個地點。在這兩個場所工作的員工也已經獲得指示繼續正常工作，以免引起歹徒的猜疑。我們要逮捕威爾森，阻止他再把任何政府機密販售給恐怖組織。」萊理說。

「那麥可會怎樣？」淚流滿面的莎拉問。

「他會沒事的，布洛德太太，這一點我們會做到！」萊理和善地說。

電子郵件

• 你使用電子郵件嗎？你有自己的帳號？你寄電子郵件給誰？你使用下列的哪些資源呢？請勾選，並與全班分享你的答案。

☐社交網路 ☐照片分享網路
☐聊天程式 ☐音樂分享網路
☐部落格

麥可飛入

P. 72

麥可飛到一個高度之後，低頭往下看。他可以看到廂型車停在樹林中，但卻看不到那幫歹徒。他開始朝高牆飛去。他在腦海中思索計畫的每個細節，他要等到晚上十點的鐘聲響起才能行動。警衛換班需要十五分鐘，在這個空檔，大樓外不會有任何人，而這正是他飛入的時刻。

他稍微降低飛行的高度，接著在空中盤旋等候。鐘響後一分鐘，他看到警衛開始走離崗哨，他馬上迅速飛越牆壁，降落在目標大樓旁的地面上。那裡有個標示寫著「總部」。他低聲對著麥克風說話。

「我到大樓的外面了。」

「很好，現在繞到大門去。」（威爾森的聲音）

庭院的燈光很明亮，麥可的全身抖得不停，心想：「我一定會被看到的。」

「我到大門了。」

「很好。現在在大門的數字鍵盤上輸入我唸給你的數字。準備好了嗎？7-8-5-0-7-9-9。」

「按好了。」

P. 74

「現在按『Enter』鍵。」

麥可按下 Enter 鍵，聽到卡嗒一聲。

「門開了。」

「很好。現在走進去，依照我的指示行動。等你拿到『獅子』信封出來後，再跟我通話。」

麥可知道一旦進入後，就必須飛上眼前走廊的天花板。他要去的辦公室在走廊的盡頭，他得飛起來，因為在走廊較低的牆面上，裝有與警報系統連線的電子感應器。

他慢慢推開門。讓他吃驚的是，他看到走廊正中央站著一位穿軍服的男人，而且手中握著一張大牌子，寫著：

麥可，不要說話！
沒事了。
警方在這裡。
你可以走到辦公室。
警報已經解除。

P. 75

這個男人笑了笑，麥可也以微笑回應。他走向走廊深處來到辦公室，在這裡有一位穿著制服的警察，手中也拿著一塊牌子，寫著：

麥可，不要說話！
從櫃子裡拿出信封
信封裡面有追蹤器
桌上還有一個追蹤器
把它放到你的口袋裡

麥可找到信封，連同追蹤器一起放入口袋。他向警察開心地揮手，然後走出辦公室，進入走廊。這兩天來，他第一次不再感到如此恐懼。當他踏入戶外來到庭院時，又有兩個警察對他微笑，並朝他比出雙手大拇指向上的手勢。麥可對著麥克風說，「我拿到『獅子』信封了。」

「太好了，馬上飛回來見我們！」威爾森說。

他振動翅膀，高高飛起越過了燈光。他知道必須按計畫行事，才不會引起他們三個人的懷疑。在飛越高牆那一刻，他心裡又開始感到害怕了。

喜兒蘭島上的好消息

P. 76

「我們找到了他！」萊理警探講完最後一通電話後，回到客廳興奮地對布洛德夫婦說。

「真是太好了！他現在在哪？」莎拉說。

「他跟歹徒在一起，不過警方給了他追蹤器，所以不管他到哪裡，我們都能掌握。」萊理回答。

「他為什麼又回去歹徒身邊？這樣不是很危險嗎？」莎拉問。

「布洛德太太，我們一定要逮捕這些人，他們能帶領警方循線揪出恐怖分子。所以我們還不能救出麥可，我們需要他。」萊理警探說。

「天啊，所以他一點也不安全，你們打算利用他找出那些恐怖分子。」莎拉說。

「對不起，布洛德太太，請你體諒我們這麼做是為了國家安全，也許還能維護世界安全。我們得馬上逮捕這些人才行。」萊理回答。

萊理警探

- 你認為萊理警探的做法正確嗎？莎拉是怎麼認為的？
- 想像一下你是萊理警探，並向夥伴說明你的計畫。

赴約

P. 77

麥可飛回歹徒躲藏的地方。

「在這裡！」他邊說，邊把「獅子」信封交出去。

「乖孩子！你表現得很好。」威爾森笑著說。接著轉身對彼得斯與杭特說：「各位，現在咱們出發去見朋友吧！」

「這男孩怎麼辦？」彼得斯問。

「我們帶在身邊，以防萬一。把他綁起來！卸下他的腰帶、麥克風和耳機，再把他塞入箱子裡。我可不想冒任何風險，現在很可能全國上下都在找他。你們把他放入廂型車後，馬上換回正常的衣服。」威爾森回答。

傑夫 • 杭特在地上挖了一個洞，掩埋他們的黑衣褲和頭套，然後上了廂型車。

「去哪兒？瘦皮猴。」負責開車的彼得斯問。

「往南開，沿著 M62 號高速公路的指標開，然後再往西。我們去曼徹斯特機場。我跟客戶約定明天早上六點碰面，所以我們時間很充裕。小心慢慢開。我現在要睡一下，離機場十英里時再叫醒我。」威爾森回答。

P. 78

午夜剛過，他們開上高速公路。威爾森仍在沉睡，杭特看著窗外，心裡擔心到底麥可知不知道他的身分？彼得斯則一直想著他能分到的酬勞：一百萬英鎊！三個人都沒有留意到後方跟著兩輛深藍色的車子，也沒聽到直昇機在他們上方飛行的聲音。

離機場 10 英里時，彼得斯大叫：「起床！瘦皮猴！我們快到了。」

P. 79

威爾森打了哈欠伸懶腰，看了看高速公路上的路標。「好，彼得斯，其實我們不是要去機場。我跟客戶約在葛蘭飯店碰面，待會你就會看到指往飯店的路標。」他說。

快到機場前三英里，他們開下高速公路，穿越一塊飯店、停車場和倉庫林立的區域。

「在那裡！」杭特說，手指向一間屋頂閃爍著「葛蘭飯店」亮眼霓虹燈的大型正方形建築。

「沒錯，彼得斯，現在開進停車場，找個安靜的地方停好，但不要離太遠，我要看到飯店門口才行。」威爾森說。

P. 80

彼得斯停好車，瘦皮猴威爾森看了看手錶，說道：「很好，快三點了。我上週在這裡訂了一間客房，在客戶抵達之前，我要先上去洗個澡，打扮體面一點再來見客戶。你們兩個可以待在車子裡，不過記得罩子放亮點。彼得斯，把槍準備好，以免有什麼狀況發生。交易完後，我們再碰面。」

他提著裝有「獅子」信封的公事包，穿過停車場，跨入飯店的玻璃大門。

就在威爾森上樓沖澡的同時，兩輛深藍色的汽車開入了飯店的停車場，一輛停在入口對面，另一輛停在他們的廂型車對面。

清晨五點，彼得斯和杭特正在車裡打瞌睡。一輛側面印著「會議籌辦」的白色大廂型車，在飯店入口外停了下來。一大群穿著白色衣袍的人下車，打開後車門，卸下一堆板子、標示等各種裝備之後，把全部的東西扛進了飯店大廳。

「發生什麼事？」彼得斯驚醒問道。

杭特打哈欠說：「噢，看起來好像飯店今天有一場會議。你看他們在門口上方掛的旗幟，寫著『第三屆《今日外科》期刊全國會議』，參加的人一定都是醫生。這種飯店常常辦這樣的活動。」

P. 81

白色廂型車裡的人

- 你想白色廂型車裡的人是誰？
  1. 是會議的工作人員
  2. 是警方的人員
  3. 是恐怖分子
- 你想接下來會發生什麼事情？

「希望他們趕快把廂型車開走，要不然我們根本看不到裡面的狀況。」彼得斯說。

他們倆一直看著那些工作人員把廂型車上的貨物卸下。五點四十五分，廂型車開走，停到了飯店後方。

「還有 15 分鐘，你看，威爾森在那裡！」彼得斯說。

杭特看到瘦皮猴威爾森站在飯店入口，眼神望向停車場。他穿著一件體面的西裝，手裡提著公事包。突然間他回頭走進飯店，對櫃臺人員說了一些話，然後走到沙發坐了下來。

「他在等聯絡人來，帶著我們白花花的鈔票出現！」彼得斯說。

P. 82

「沒錯，我口袋裡已經有一張到美國的

機票了！待會我要坐十一點的飛機離開這裡，然後下午四點再從倫敦希斯洛機場搭機到紐約。再見了英國！奢華的新生活，我來囉！」杭特說。

兩人大笑。他們看到許多汽車和廂型車開進停車場，把大部分的車位都停滿了。許多穿黑西裝的男人下車，走向飯店入口。

「今天早上這裡還真忙，你說是不是？太多人了，我不喜歡。」彼得斯說。

「別擔心啦，彼得斯，他們只是來開會的。」杭特說。

決戰時刻

P. 83

這天凌晨五點半，一架警方的直昇機降落曼徹斯特機場，沒有引起任何人注意。也沒有人看到萊理警探、布洛德夫婦跳下直昇機，鑽入一輛沒有識別、正在等候他們的藍色警車。

當這輛車子開入葛蘭飯店的停車場後沒多久，萊理警探向布洛德夫婦說明眼前的情況。「你們有看到那些穿白色袍子的人嗎？他們都是警察，假扮成籌辦會議的工作人員。麥可就在右邊那輛白色電腦廂型車裡，有兩個歹徒陪著他，而威爾森正在飯店裡等候核子機密的買家。」

P. 84

「我不知道機場飯店在清晨這個時段這麼繁忙，你看那些人！。」

萊理笑著說：「布洛德太太，他們也是警察，假扮成前來參加會議的醫生。我們計畫叫全部的警察擠滿飯店接待區，讓威爾森跟他的客戶無法脫逃。」

「就好像電視上的驚悚節目一樣。」喬治笑著說。

五點五十九分，一輛黑色豪華轎車開到飯店外停下。一位穿著典雅的紳士提著公事包走下車。他來到飯店櫃臺，找接待人員講話，接待人員隨即指向坐在沙發上的瘦皮猴威爾森。威爾森站起身，露出微笑，兩人相互握手後坐下，開始交談。

約莫一、兩分鐘後，威爾森從公事包抽出獅子信封，交給對方，對方將公事包放在面前的咖啡桌上，兩人再度握手。突然間，不知從何處冒出了二、三十個人，有的穿西裝，有的穿袍子，迅速包圍了威爾森和另一個人——他們兩人毫無逃脫的機會。他們被銬上手銬，帶到飯店後方的一個房間。

在此同時，來了更多警察團團圍住停車場裡的黑色豪華轎車，其他的警察則拉開電腦廂型車的所有車門，坐在車裡的杭特和彼得斯嚇得啞口無言。警方把兩人帶到在停車場等候的一輛藍色廂型車裡。

P. 86

萊理和布洛德夫婦立刻奔向電腦廂型車，警探找到了鑰匙，打開後車門。

「麥可！麥可，你在哪裡？」他大喊。

「在這裡。」箱子裡傳來了隱約的聲音。

兩名警察小心翼翼把箱子抬出車外，放在地上打開。清晨陽光射入了麥可的眼睛，他眨了眨眼，過了好幾分鐘才看清楚站在他周遭、帶著微笑的所有人。

「麥可！麥可！」莎拉是第一個開口的人，她緊緊將麥可抱在懷裡，喬治隨即抱住他們兩人。

「你還好嗎？」喬治問。

「嗯，我很好。」麥可說，臉上露出了燦爛的笑容，「不過，誰可以幫我解開翅膀的繩子嗎？」

「啊，麥可，你漂亮的白色羽毛怎麼了？」莎拉大聲地問。

「別擔心，莎拉，那只是染料而已，很快就會褪掉的。」麥可雙手緊緊抱著她回答。

麥可和布洛德夫婦並沒有立即返回喜兒蘭。他們在曼徹斯特上等飯店裡的豪華套房住了一個星期，因為警方需要對麥可進行偵訊。住在飯店期間，他們看到了電視上播映《奇情人間》介紹麥可的節目。在這星期結束的前兩天，大家都在討論麥可的未來。有太多事情等著下決定。

布洛德夫婦、麥可和李德醫生飛回喜兒蘭時有兩名警察陪同。他們是麥可的終身保鑣，這樣麥可整個夏季都能盡情地放鬆、愉快地生活。很快地，八月底到來，又該是麥可搬家的時候了。

結語

P. 88

九月初，布洛德夫婦和麥可搬到英格蘭北方的一個村莊，麥可進入當地的中學就讀三年級。人們沒有問太多問題便接納了他，很快他就結交了很多朋友。他在十八歲時，事情出現了變化，喬治過世了，而麥可也開始進入大學主修生物學。他取得優異的學位，接著繼續攻讀碩士，論文題目是研究喜兒蘭島上的稀有花卉。

後來，他返回英格蘭的村莊，陪莎拉一起生活。莎拉過世之後，麥可在他的中學母校擔任教生物學的工作。學生很喜歡他的飛行課，因為他會帶學生到操場進行現場示範。

大約每週一次，他會在四下無人、不被瞧見時飛上天空，享受遨翔的快樂。

李德醫生仍和他保持聯絡，每隔三個月就會來探視他，記錄他所有的細微變化。現在，我們要讓這位會飛的男子回到我們最初發現他的地方囉：他正穿越公園，準備回家吃晚餐！

ANSWER KEY

Before Reading

Page 6

2

a) House Sparrow
b) Ostrich
c) Emperor Penguin
d) Eagle Owl
e) Emperor Penguin
f) Eagle Owl (House Sparrows and Ostriches also eat insects and small vertebrates but these are not part of their primary diet)
g) Emperor Penguin
h) Emperor Penguin and Ostrich

Page 7

3 a) wings b) feather
4 a) 3 b) 1 c) 2
5 Daedalus and Icarus

Page 9

10 (Possible answer)

a) Three people – a man, a woman and a child – are approaching a castle. The child has wings. They are walking and seem to be in the middle of the countryside. There is a peaceful and relaxed atmosphere.
b) The picture is inside a room. There are three men wearing dark clothes and balaclavas. The boy from Picture a) is tied to a chair. He is a prisoner. There is very little furniture in the room and the atmosphere is tense.

Page 11

12

a) Jeff, Wilson and Peters.
b) No, they didn't kill him.
c) They carried him to Laird's Wood.

Page 15

- Aristotle was a Greek philosopher.
- Charles Dickens was a British author.
- Crazy Horse was a leader of the Oglala Lakota tribe of Native Americans.
- Edgar Allan Poe was an American author.
- John Lennon was a British singer and songwriter.
- Nelson Mandela is a South African statesman and humanitarian.

Page 46

- Wilson knows that Michael is on Shillan because Michael uses the preposition 'on' and you only use 'on' when you talk about hills or islands.

Page 47

a) in b) at c) at/beside d) at
e) in f) on g) in h) on

Page 76

- Sarah doesn't think that Detective Riley did the correct thing.

After Reading

Page 92

7 (Possible answer)

b) He is the sound and lighting technician who finds out where Michael lives.
c) He is the doctor who looks after Michael's health and studies his development.

d) He is the producer of the program *Strange But True*.
e) He is an international criminal.
f) He is the police officer who is on Michael's case.

8 (Possible answer)
- The doctors keep Michael at the hospital because they want to study him. Michael doesn't like being there.

Page 93

10 (Possible answer)
- When Michael gets home there are a crowd of journalists and paparazzi waiting for him. Then the doctor and two policemen arrive.

11 (Possible answer)
- Michael's life on Shillan is very solitary.

12 (Possible answer)
- The gang discovered where Michael lived because one of them took part in the filming of a documentary about Michael and he managed to get Michael to give him a clue about where he lived.

13 (Possible answer)
- Wilson wanted Michael to steal an envelope containing secret documents which he wants to sell to a group of terrorists.

14 (Possible answer)
- There are soldiers inside the building holding signs with instructions for Michael.

15 (Possible answer)
- Wilson goes to the Grand Hotel, beside Manchester Airport where he has a meeting with the people who want to buy the stolen documents.

16 (Possible answer)
- There is a tracking device in the envelope and another one in Michael's pocket.

17 (Possible answer)
- The policemen pretend that they are setting up a conference inside the hotel and surround the men.

Page 94

19

a) Because there is a piece of paper with the name Michael written on it inside the basket where Sarah found him.
b) Edward.
c) John.
d) Mary is the person who interviews him for the television program.
e) Mr Smith teaches Michael about flight and flying at the hospital.
f) He is called Pete, and he teaches Michael exercises to make his chest muscles stronger when Michael is at the hospital.
g) They are Michael's online tutors.

20
- Sarah is important in the story as she is Michael's mother. Slim Wilson is important because he is the villain who kidnaps Michael. The other characters are not central to the story.

21 (Possible answer)
- Michael is happy when he arrives on Shillan and while he is living there. He is not happy when he is in the hospital.

Page 95

22

a) Michael says this to the doctors at the hospital when he wants to leave.

b) The doctor says this to George and Sarah after they help Michael to escape from the hospital.
c) Dr Reed says this to George, Sarah and Michael after the BBC contact his boss.
d) Jeff Hunter says this to Michael while they are having a break from filming.
e) Peters says this to Hunter while they are waiting for Wilson outside the Grand Hotel.
f) Sarah says this to Michael when he is freed.

Page 96

25 a) 2 b) 4 c) 1 d) 3

26 (Possible answer)
a) They are walking across the airport.
b) He is holding a sign up to Michael.
c) They are shouting at Michael.
d) He is sitting with his hands tied together.

27
- b) The characters are described from a third person point of view throughout.

Page 97

28 (Possible answer)
- They are set in present time. The rest of the book is in the past. This gives the idea of the story being real and continuing.

29 (Possible answer)
- Michael grows wings.
- Michael moves to hospital.
- Michael escapes from hospital.
- Michael and his parents move to Shillan.
- The BBC makes a documentary about Michael.
- Michael is kidnapped.
- Michael steals secret documents for his kidnappers.

Page 98

34
a) air (n.)
b) feather (v.)
c) hover (v.)
d) wing (n.)
e) flight (n.)
f) fly (v.)

35
a) flew
b) rose
c) opened
d) hovered
e) landed

36
b) Dr Reed filmed Michael doing his exercises every day.
c) Michael was very interested in Biology.
d) The police discovered where Wilson's gang was.
e) Wilson wanted Michael to take an envelope.
f) Sarah made special clothes for Michael.

Page 99

37
a) happy
b) beautiful
c) rare
d) worried
e) frightened

38
b) gently
c) silently
d) immediately
e) suddenly
f) obviously

39

a) What did Sarah do on Shillan?
b) When did Michael grow wings?
c) How did Michael escape from hospital?
d) What did Wilson want Michael to steal?
e) Who discovered where Michael lived?

Test

Page 100

1

a) 3 subject
b) 3 interested
c) 1 study
d) 2 flew
e) 3 saving
f) 3 wasn't
g) 1 popular
h) 3 showed

Page 101

3

a) F b) F c) T d) F
e) F f) F g) T e) F

國家圖書館出版品預行編目資料

飛翔吧，男孩 / David A. Hill 著；李俊忠 譯．一初版．一[臺北市]：寂天文化，2012.6
面；公分．

中英對照

ISBN 978-986-318-002-9 (25K 平裝附光碟片)

1. 英語　2. 讀本

805.18　101008229

■作者 _ David A. Hill ■譯者 _ 李俊忠 ■校對 _ 陳慧莉
■封面設計 _ 蔡怡柔 ■主編 _ 黃鈺云 ■製程管理 _ 蔡智堯
■出版者 _ 寂天文化事業股份有限公司 ■電話 _ 02-2365-9739 ■傳真 _ 02-2365-9835
■網址 _ www.icosmos.com.tw ■讀者服務 _ onlineservice@icosmos.com.tw
■出版日期 _ 2012年6月 初版一刷（250101）
■郵撥帳號 _ 1998620-0 寂天文化事業股份有限公司
■訂購金額600（含）元以上郵資免費 ■訂購金額600元以下者，請外加郵資60元